CHINCOTEAGUE SUMMER OF 1948

# CHINCOTEAGUE SUMMER OF 1948

## A Waterman's Childhood Stories

### Ed Waterhouse

iUniverse, Inc.
New York  Lincoln  Shanghai

## Chincoteague Summer of 1948
A Waterman's Childhood Stories

All Rights Reserved © 2003 by Edward W. Waterhouse

No part of this book may be reproduced or transmitted in any form or by any means, graphic, electronic, or mechanical, including photocopying, recording, taping, or by any information storage retrieval system, without the written permission of the publisher.

iUniverse, Inc.

For information address:
iUniverse, Inc.
2021 Pine Lake Road, Suite 100
Lincoln, NE 68512
www.iuniverse.com

ISBN: 0-595-29941-5

Printed in the United States of America

# Contents

Preface .................................................................................... vii
Session One (Recorded July 6, 1999) ..................................... 1
Session Two (Recorded July 13, 1999) ................................... 8
Session Three (Recorded July 20, 1999) ............................... 17
Session Four (Recorded July 27, 1999) ................................. 26
Session Five (Recorded August 3, 1999) ............................... 33
Session Six (Recorded August 10, 1999) ............................... 41
Session Seven (Recorded August 17, 1999) .......................... 46
Session Eight (Recorded August 24, 1999) ........................... 51
Session Nine (Recorded August 31, 1999) ............................ 57
Session Ten (Recorded September 7, 1999) .......................... 64
Epilogue ................................................................................ 73

# Preface

I was born on Chincoteague Island, Virginia, probably known to the reader for its wild pony roundup made famous by Marguerite Henry's book, *Misty of Chincoteague*. Although I have not resided there since high school, I have not lost my interest in that lovely island and its native residents. I realized that the number of residents with long unbroken genealogical ties to Chincoteague is decreasing rapidly. This realization led me, in the summer of 1999, to record a series of oral histories narrated by elderly Chincoteague Island natives. This book chronicles the recollections of how things were during the Summer of 1948 as told by one of those Chincoteaguers, Thurston Watson, a fascinating character, by far the most interesting of all those I recorded. None of the others I recorded had Thurston Watson's flair for story-telling. His stories of his idyllic childhood during the summer of 1948 on Chincoteague Island were to me, spellbinding.

I felt very lucky to find him. I had made it a habit to ask my narrators to recommend others who might be willing to record their memoirs, and one elderly widow suggested I might find "a Chincoteaguer or two" in a certain nursing home in Parksley, Virginia, a town on the mainland not far from Chincoteague, and there I found Mr. Watson. He was the only person I recorded who had spent virtually all of his working life as what natives on the Eastern Shore of Virginia call a waterman, a person who earns a living selling seafood he personally harvests from the local waters. Most of my subjects were women, island men dying younger than the women as a rule, and although the women's recollections were relevant and provided many details of daily household life, they seldom included intricate details of their men's work.

There are few watermen today. The individual waterman, his work schedule dependent on favorable weather and tides, his seafood harvest changing with the seasons, has largely been replaced by machines that ignore all but the worst weather as they efficiently savage the waterways in their attempt to meet the ever-increasing world-wide demand for seafood. In addition, the explosion of motorboat ownership and the ability to trailer those boats to fishing spots far away has crowded the waterways with sports fishermen. The resulting depletion of the seafood resource has led to state-created regulator bureaucracies that limit collection of seafood by sportsmen and professional watermen alike. These limitations merely cause sport fishermen to reschedule their pleasure trips or to release undersized catches, but to professional watermen, every conservation regulation diminishes the opportunity to profit, reducing the attractiveness of waterman as a profession. Few youths today opt for waterman as a life vocation. The art, science, and details of the profession of waterman are being lost.

I was pleasantly surprised at how little it took to convince Mr. Watson to narrate these memoirs. On meeting him, I expressed my belief that his recollections would contribute to the history of Chincoteague and help preserve the details of the profession of waterman, and he agreed to record weekly, with one condition: I was to bring him an uncooled bottle of RC Cola for each session.

"All they serves in this here old folks home is Coke and Pepsi. But I always been a RC man. I drunk so much of it they would a called me RC for a nickname but another boy, one a the Boone boys, as I recall, was already nicknamed RC for similar reasons. Besides, they always serves soft drinks ice cold here but I like my RC warm. More flavorful," he explained.

I agreed to his condition. Each Tuesday when I sat with him at the institution's dining room table for our afternoon meeting, I opened my briefcase, removed my portable cassette recorder, pencils, a legal pad, and finally, a warm bottle of RC Cola. I removed its cap very slowly so the warm cola would not fizz out, then I pushed the bottle across the table to him. Mr. Watson clenched his skinny fingers with their swelled arthritic joints around the greenish glass bottle, wiped its opening with his other palm and chugged down half of the twelve ounces. He had no teeth. He suckled at the bottle, his lips barely maintaining their flabby contact with it. As his cheeks saucered concave with each suck, and his prominent Adam's Apple bobbed with each swallow, rippling the wattle between his prominent neck tendons. Sometimes a rivulet of cola dribbled from a corner of his mouth and down his blue-hued clean-shaven jaw, but he never allowed it to reach his flannel gown, sopping it with a quick swipe of a neatly folded red handkerchief he whipped from the gown's breast pocket. He signaled his readiness to begin recording by wiping his mouth with a theatrical swipe of the back of his hand and emitting a resounding belch.

Mr. Watson's lifelong exposure to the elements had given him a deep mahogany tan that intensified the platinum white of his close-cropped hair, which was thinner in the region of his widow's peak. That tan, combined with the clear whites of his eyes made him look healthy, though I came to realize he was not. The hairs atop his head were stark against that leathery tan, and the fuzz on the sides of his head was so thin that I could distinguish individual hairs. His wrinkles were deep and permanent, so deep they did not appear to decrease in depth when they were stretched, as when he smiled. A slender man, he spoke in an unexpectedly deep, strong bass, like a radio announcer, but his Chincoteague accent, malapropisms and mispronunciations quickly destroyed that illusion. Like many watermen, he had developed cataracts early in life and the thick spectacles he wore magnified his intense blue eyes. A wisp of white hair protruding from each ear and his white eyebrows, each with a central tuft pointing upward, combined to make him look impish. Each time we met he was dressed in nursing home unwrinkled blue pajamas, a plaid flannel robe, and plaid cloth bedroom slippers and, in contrast to most of the other residents, he looked dapper. He was of average height but his thin frame made him look tall, and he strode when he walked. Proudly, it seemed to me. At each meeting, we shook hands, and at each I felt his clasp grow weaker, though his voice and memory continued strong.

He was genteel in an old-fashioned way, for example politely rising when a lady, even the scrub woman, entered the room, or raising two fingers to his forehead as though touching the brim of an imaginary hat when someone walked past as we strode the hall from the reception area to the dining room. He addressed all women as "Ma'am" and all men, including me, as "Sir". The longer I associated with him, the more I came to like and admire him. He had such a gregarious personality that I was amazed when the receptionist told me I was the only visitor Mr. Watson had ever received. In my experience, I have found elderly native Chincoteaguers generally distrustful of "mainlanders" and others outside their circle of island acquaintances, though they were open to other Chincoteaguers, often to the point of impertinence. I attribute both the distrustfulness and the impertinence to the relative isolation of the islanders for so many years.

He was always well prepared for our sessions. I believe he secretly rehearsed what he was going to narrate, for he never hesitated nor stopped to gather his thoughts as did many of my narrators. He wove a fact-filled, informative oral history, but he did occasionally stray from his story line, sometimes recalling and injecting facts relating to a previous session, or repeating and embellishing a prior story, so I have edited some parts, but only those few I felt would make it easier for the reader to follow. Occasionally, if I raised my eyebrows at something he had just narrated, he would give me a smile and a lingering wink, which I took as acknowledgment that the statement was an exaggeration. Nevertheless, I left it in the history, because it was his history, not my interpretation of his history. When telling his stories, Mr. Watson seemed to transport himself back in time, using words and phrases in common use in 1948, and he swept me there with him. He was a great actor.

I caution the reader that Mr. Watson uses words and phrases that today may offend, but I believe they are typical of those used by many elderly Chincoteagers, and certainly are typical of words and phrases used in 1948 on Chincoteague Island. In truth I cannot say if he was or was not racially biased, but if he was, I saw no sign of it in his relations with persons of color we encountered at the home.

I have phonetically spelled many, though not all, of Mr. Watson's words to give you a taste of the Chincoteague *patois*. Chincoteaguers, when traveling, are frequently mistaken for Canadians when they speak. The unique Chincoteague accent came with the settlers who also populated Nova Scotia. Indeed, if you listened to a Nova Scotian today, you would hear a very similar accent, both regions' isolation through the years having conserved it. The most striking feature of this accent is the pronunciation of the word *out*, and all words that rhyme with it, and the word *house*, and all its rhymes. I have heard would-be imitators pronounce *out* to rhyme with *coot* and *house* to rhyme with *moose*. Neither is close to the Chincoteague Islander pronunciation, and I regret that I find it impossible to describe their pronunciation of those words with absolute accuracy, but to my ear, their *out* sounds like the French pronunciation of their word for August: *Aout*, and their pronunciation of *house* to me sounds like it rhymes with *louse*, but my ear for the Chincoteaguers' pronunciation may be flawed by having the same accent myself.

Also, Mr. Watson's particular way with words included the frequent use of the word *kindly* by which he meant *kind of*. His other language peculiarities are easier to translate, so I leave them to the reader to untangle.

I hope you enjoy *Summer of '48*. It is Thurston Watson's own story, warts and all, in his own words, with (I suspect) an occasional Thurston Watson exaggeration. We recorded ten sessions covering his memories of the summer of 1948. I wish we could have recorded more, but Mr. Watson died two days after narrating the tenth. The nursing home notified me, and I attended his last rites. There was a small gathering of patients and staff at the memorial service in the nursing home's chapel. Except for a Baptist preacher from nearby Parksley, who gave

Thurston Watson as good a send-off as one could expect, I was the only outsider in the tiny chapel.

Ed Waterhouse
San Diego, California

# Session One
## (Recorded July 6, 1999)
### About Meself

"That thing on, sir? My name is Thurston Watson. I was born on January the third of Our Lord's Year nineteen and thirty-six on Chincoteague Island, County of Accomack, Commonwealth of Virginia. Nobody gave me no middle name, but for a nickname, folks mostly call me Thirsty, because it kindly goes with my given name of Thurston and also signifies that I am always thirsty for a RC Cola.

I have been thinking on how to tell you the facts about how my life was in the summer of forty-eight, and I recall from my limited schooling just how boring it was just to say a bunch a facts, so I decided to let my story flow natural as best I can, and as I come to something needs a explanation, why, I will do it right then. If it becomes burdensome to read, I am sure this nice feller with the recording machine will work on it and make it better.

But right now at the outset I will have to give you some facts that I don't think would fit well if told right in the middle of a exciting story, facts like background about meself, some history, some geography and some other things I think you might need to know so's you can easier foller what comes later. I hope you will forgive me if I confuse a event or two, or a location or two on or off the island, or if I am off in my dates, or even the year sometimes, but all that I will say about that is that a soul's recall abilities fades as he gets older and I will be telling you things to my best recollection.

I am, like my daddy was, and his daddy was, a waterman. I quit school as soon as it was legal to do it, at age sixteen, feeling I had got enough schooling by then to read and write and to figger good enough to keep the man buying my clams honest and to keep the tax man away. In my lifetime I have done just about everthing a body can do to make a living on the water, and I will now describe some of the ways us watermen made our living.

One way I made my living was clamming. Right after the big war with Hitler and Tojo, seems to me a waterman would get maybe one cent apiece for large clams and two cent apiece for the smaller and tastier little nick and cherrystone clams, and a good day's work might bring in fifteen or twenty dollar before expenses. That gave a waterman a right good living at a time many folks was getting thirty-five to fifty cent an hour for dry-land work, but a falling glass bringing unclement weather sometimes made it unfit to be on the water, and expenses such as boat maintenance, cotton flannel to sew up into new clamming moccasins, and other incidentals et up some of that money and brought watermen's wages down to probably about the same level as dry-land wages. As for clams, I raked 'em, signed 'em, and waded 'em. Even stole some from Charley Hancock's clam bed till one day he drawed a bead on me with his twelve gauge scattergun. That happened when I was right young and left me with the unevitable feeling that honest work was considerable less dangerous than the outlaw life.

When I first started clamming for my living, you did not have to go too far to find plenty of clams. Sometimes good pickings was so close I could see my house on South Main Street while I was clamming, but as time passed, things ganged up on clammers. The good places would get clammed out, or the state man would put parts of Chincoteague Channel or the bays closed to clamming on account of polelution, so watermen had to go futher and futher away from home to get enough clams to make a living. After a while it become so far to go that your day was wasted sculling your bateau to and from your day's work. Then we would find a man with a motorboat who would tow us up the bay or down the bay, wherever we thought the clams was thick. He did it for a percentage of our clam-pile, or some would do it for a flat dollar amount per trip. Some of them did a right good job of it, cooking up a nice lunch for the clammers or once in a while providing a sip of coffee or water, in general making life somewhat comfortable for the clammers, at least as comfortable as you can get while soaking wet.

Them motorboats they towed us with was long scows, maybe twenty or twenty-five foot, some with a little dead-rise to ease the wave chop. They had what I call a stoop cabin, you could not stand up in it, covering the engine compartment aft. That aft cabin was there mainly to protect the engine, though a soul could get out of the rain or the wind in there to let the engine heat kindly take the chill off of a cold day. The scows had a open hold all the way from the cabin, which was astern, to the bow, leaving plenty of room for everbody to put their clams, ever clammer's pile separated from everbody else's by boards like bundling boards on Pilgrim beds in the history books. Steering the boat was by a tiller on the starboard side that connected to the rudder with ropes and pulleys. Pull the tiller aft, boat turns to starboard, push it for'ds, boat goes to port. Seems to me most of them scows was painted green. I don't know why. Could have been green paint was cheaper or it could have been convention.

Early of a morning you might see a couple of them clamboats, each with a long single file tow of watermen's scows and bateaus, many as eight or ten boats being pulled by each motorboat, each waterman getting his gear set up or maybe sitting on the stern of his boat puffing on a morning Marvel cigarette or a pipeful of Prince Albert t'baccer, maybe sipping coffee from a Mason jar or a Thermos jug, if they could afford one. With the sun rising up and casting gold splashes across the smooth and glassy water, it was right picturest.

Raking clams is pulling a rake with real long thin tines through the mud or sand and when you hear and feel something sounds kindly like scratching fingernails across a slate blackboard, you got a clam there. You can rake clams from the high water line of the shore out to maybe chest-high in the water, though waist-high water is about my personal comfort limit for raking clams.

Signing clams is looking for what looks like a tiny keyhole in the sand or mud, caused by the way a clam eats, sucking in water in one hole, straining food out of it and blowing that water out another hole right next to the in-hole, him being a bivalve. Often the out-hole has some tiny clam turds next to it. You can sign clams from the high water mark on the shore out to shin-deep or shallier water, main limitation being how well you can see the clear bottom. Wind causing ripples on the water can make it near impossible to sign clams in water much above your ankles. Signing is hard on the back because you bent over looking for them keyholes. Sometimes when you walking along looking, the clam feels you coming and snaps his shell shut, thinking that'll make him safer, but him closing squirts a little puff of mud out of his out-hole and that gives his hiding place away. Dig a couple inch under the sign, either the keyhole or the clam turds or the mud puff, you got a clam there. Clams signs better the hotter it gets. Watermen used to say "How they signing?" as a greeting, like saying "Howdy."

The men being towed up the bay was likely going to be wading clams. You wade clams leaning on the side of your bateau in water where you can reach bottom with your feet. You wear homemade cotton flannel moccasins with the fuzzy side out to protect your feet from getting cut on the occasional sharp shell, though a professional clam wader's feet is right tough. You slide your feet around in the mud like you're dancing a Bojangles sand-dance, till you feel the edge of a clam buried in the mud. You dig him out of his hole with your toes. Then you slides that clam up the inside of your leg using your other leg's toes and you reach down with your hand and pluck the clam off of your leg. Another way of bringing up the clams takes more practice but is faster: you pack the clam on top of your other foot with mud and bring your knee to your chin, balancing the clam till you get aholt of it with your hand, swish it in the water a couple times to clean off the mud, and add 'er to your pile. Sometimes wading clams, you might get a surprise when you step on a bullfish, or a skate, or a hoss-shoe crab, all three of which is competing with you for them clams.

When wading or raking clams, watermen wore clothes, often a couple of pair of union suit long johns. Kept 'em warm kindly like them sport snorkeler's rubber suits do today.

One last thing I might mention about clams: Old Chincoteaguers call a woman's thing her clam due to what they precieve as a right close resemblance, and they call a man's thing a wilk for the same reason.

Crabbing is mostly done by using traps called pots, which you bait with trash fish, attracting crabs to crawl into the trap through a cone-entrance. Crabs ain't too smart. They have a lot of trouble finding their way back out that same hole, or maybe they just want to stay near the free lunch. You make your crab pots out of galvanized chicken wire. Even galvanized chicken wire gets et up in no time by rust in salt water, so you put a zinc block on ever pot and the salt water eats away that zinc instead of rusting the wire. Right interesting thing.

You sets out your crab pots where your experience tells you there might be crabs. Where a gut flows into the channel might be such a place. Next day you gets the crabs out of them pots, freshens the bait and sets 'em out again. You fish your pots at least ever forty-eight hours, another enviromeddler rule, I expect. Ever one of your pots got a float painted with your special colors at the end of a length of rope so you can find your pots and not fish somebody else's by mistake. Colors don't do much good keeping them city tourists out of your traps, though. Some of them seem to think they got salvage rights on your pots.

Also, instead of bait, at the right time of the month, you can tie a rank Jimmy crab in the bait compartment and the female crabs will come to him because they in heat.

Another way of crabbing is trot-lining. You attach salt pork rind skins ever six foot or so on a roll of twenty pound number one cotton line by untwisting the lay, inserting the pork skin and twisting the lay back into position, making it look like you got a pork skin bow tie ever six foot, and you runs out two or three, many as you think you can fish, of them four hundred and fifty yard balls of that baited line tied end to end. You put a concrete block anchor and a flag marker on each extreme end so folks won't cut your trot line with one of them stern-kicker motors. Then you sets the line in a notch in a pole protruding off the side of your bateau and slow cruise along the line from one flag to the other, over and over. Got to keep your bateau cruising straight along the line or the line gets stretched if you off to one side and then you got a mess to get it all straight again. As you cruise along it, the line slides through the notch making the crabs fall into a basket you got hanging under the notch as the notch knocks 'em off of your baits. You throw the small crabs back overboard and for the questionable size ones, you got a gouge cut in your gunnel set to the size the state says you can keep. Trot-lining is equalnomical. You store your cotton line, bait and all, into a barrel of salt brine, we call it the pickle, when you're done that day. Salt taste don't bother crabs, they living in salt water anyhow, so everthing they eat has to taste salty. Baits lasts a long time, and if it don't, that means lot of crabs biting at it, so you don't mind buying more bait. The best trot-line bait is salt eel, but unless you catch 'em yourself, that bait is prohibitive expensive. Lazy watermen has just about stopped trot-lining as a crabbing method. Rather than having to stay on the water and tend a trot-line, they rather just let some crab pots work while they off doing something else. Used to be a separate state license to do trot-lining but there's so little call for it, the state of Virginia combined that license with the crab pot license.

Third way of crabbing is walking along in shallow water with a scoop net. Scooping was done mostly done by young'uns and housewifes picking up pin money or just getting a mess of crabs for supper. Spot a crab, scoop 'im up. Also poke the handle of your scoop net under ever piece of moss. If a crab there, he tries to get away but you scoops 'im up. Then you reach under that moss with your bare hand and gentle feel in the mud for a soft crab or a peeler who's getting ready to shed his shell. They worth lots more than regular hard shell crabs. Once in a while you will scoop up a Jimmy that is holding a female underneath his self. We call that situation a "Jimmy and his wife".

One last thing about crabs is folks says if a crab bites you he won't let go until the sun goes down. I don't know where that saying come from but one feller swears it is true. I don't remember his last name but everbody called him "Crab

Jim" from one time he was doing his number two business sitting on the gunnel of his bateau with his pants down to his knees and some of his manly parts was hanging down and a big Jimmy crab got a pincer-holt on his gonad. Sometime after, in a conversation with a friend about crabs hanging on until sunset, Crab Jim made the tactical mistake of telling about his experience on the subject, how he broke the claw off of the crab but it still clamped tight and he had a intricate experience removing the claw by crushing it with a pair of rusty pliers. Being human, Crab Jim's friend could not wait to tell somebody, so word got around and for the rest of his days folks called him Crab Jim and teased him by asking him in public where the crab bit him.

I done some eeling in my time, too. Caught 'em with fish lines, or in traps we call eel pots, and when they go down in the mud for the winter, I gigged 'em. Eels will strike at a baited hook, but only yellow bellies do that. Silver belly eels won't. Yellow bellies turn silver to spawn, then they die. Only yellow belly eels go down in the mud for the winter. On the bay side of the Eastern Shore Peninsular in the Chesapeake Bay there's pounds set up to catch eels on their way up or down that body of water. Pounds is just a net fence set up from the shore out into the water. Eel swimming along, runs into the net, goes along it to the end where he thinks he will swim around it but instead there is a pocket he can't get out of. Main buyers of eels is Squareheads from Denmark. They pay good prices for live eels, which they take back to Denmark alive in tanks, only to kill 'em over there and salt 'em or smoke 'em. Seems like to me they could save a lot of expenses by salting or smoking 'em here, but it is well knowed you can't tell no Squarehead nothing.

I can't tell you all the different ways I fished for fish, so I will just tell you the way I like the best. You go in your bateau out at night, just drifting quietly, and listen for fatback, flipping and splashing the water. You go to the noise, and you will find a school of them right close to the marsh. They won't bite a hook so you have to use a gill net. They are a oily fish, so oily that sometimes you can see a smooth oil slick on the water over a big school of them. Real quiet, you put out your gill net from the shore on one side of them all the way around that school like a great big "U" back to the shore on the other side of them. Gill net has floats on the top and lead sinkers on the bottom, making it like a fence in the water. Then you jump out of your bateau and run around inside that "U", splashing your oar on the water. That spooks them fatbacks into your gill net and you pull in your net, pick out the fish and sell 'em. Inside the mouth of some fatbacks you will find a tiny little crab who eats the same food as the fatback is straining out of the water. He is a kindly parasite. Fascinating thing.

We used to sell our fatback to a man who walked all over the island with iced fish in his pushcart. He blowed a foghorn and shouted, "Fresh fish! Fatback! Croakers!", whatever fish he had in his cart. Right convenient for all them housewifes. Weren't too many with automobiles then and many did not care to walk all the way to town to get a mess of fish for supper.

I expect that about covers the work of being a waterman, except to tell you that if you think about it, the only days a waterman took off from his work was caused by unclement weather, unless he got religion, in which case even if Sunday was a pretty day, he would still go to church services, but many of them who got religion told me it felt strange to see a nice day and not be working on the water.

Anything else comes to mind about the waterman business, I will fill you in on as the need rises. So's you can foller what I tell you later, I will tell you next week some details of how things was, how folks was, and some things I think you might need to help you foller along, such as the some history and geography."

# Session Two
## (Recorded July 13, 1999)
### History and Geography

"We recording sir? Folks today says the name Chincoteague means "Beautiful Land Across the Water" in Indian talk. That may be. But my instincts tell me that meaning was made up in the olden days by someone to get city swells to come spend their money. Speaking of city visitors, I know the dictionary don't agree with me, but I think we called 'em swells because they was always saying things like, "Ain't that swell," or, "I feel just swell."

About the "Beautiful Land Across the Water" meaning, my cousin Fay's grannie, she was full-blood Metompkin Indian, said the name Chincoteague, that Fay's grannie pronounced "Gingoteake", could have also meant "Many Smelly Piles of Oyster Shells." For reasons you will understand later, I lean to Grannie Reid's side of that argument.

Chincoteague Island is about seven mile long and a couple mile wide. West of it is several mile of channels and guts and marshes and then the mainland. I think it was in the nineteen and twenties they put a toll road made out of oyster shells across them marshes to Chincoteague with bridges spanning the channels, guts, and other waterways. Old folks still calls that road the toll road, though there hain't no toll to use it. Might have been when it was first built, but there never was a toll in my memory. Last bridge before you get to the island is a swing-open one so tall boats going up and down Chincoteague Channel can pass through.

Folks also still refers to that old swing-open bridge as the toll bridge. They going to replace that old bridge and the toll road with a highway leading more or less directly to the beach to Assateague, bypassing pretty well the whole town of Chincoteague. I figger that situation will make some folks happy that the old-timey calm might return to their neighborhoods, and it will make some people right unhappy, the unhappy ones being the town merchants, as their wages come mostly from them tourists.

North end of Chincoteague is almost in Maryland. South end is opposite Wallops Island, on the mainland, where they shoots rocket space shots, putting up satellites. A lot of foreigners comes there to shoot the rockets, Japs, Ruskies, I-talians, Squareheads, and more. Wallops is part of NASA now but when I was twelve years old, Wallops was part of a United States Navy Base where they tested bombs and guns and practiced shooting their airplane guns. That Navy Base was an airplane base, called a Naval Aviation Ordinance Test Station, which the goverment shortened to NAOTS which folks pronounced "notes" so you could say it in one breath.

A lot of the navy pilots lived to Chincoteague. They flew little airplanes, called Hellcats, Wildcats, and Corsairs, and other such exciting names. They practiced by shooting down little airplanes called drones, that had no pilots. I am knowledgeable here as I worked a couple years steaming out to the ocean where them drones was shot down, and hauling them back to be fixed up to be shot at again. We had two navy landing craft, the kind that flops down their front on the beach, connected about ten foot apart, side-by-side with steel I-beams, and a winch in the middle between the two boats. We just winched the shot down drone up between them two boats and steamed back to NAOTS with it hanging there. I forgot to tell you them drones was made out of plywood and designed to float after they was shot down and had an eyebolt on top that we hooked the winch cable to. Another way them pilots practiced shooting was with long silk targets they towed some distance behind one airplane for the other pilots to shoot at. I found one of them tow targets washed up on Assateague Beach and my momma made some right nice window curtains out of the parts of it that did not have no bullet-holes. I never envied the man flying the tow airplane. He sure have to keep on everybody's good side so as not to pick up a stray bullet.

Them pilots was hotshots, known for flying low to impress galfriends, or just showing off in general. It was called buzzing. They say Old Man George Bush, the forty-first United States President, was stationed at the base right after the big war and got chewed out by his Cap'n for buzzing a circus parade over to Crisfield, Maryland on the mainland, showing off for a galfriend. Said it scairt folks near to death when him buzzing caused a elephant stampede, although in my experience the miserable little circuses that come to miserable little places like Crisfield only had one elephant at best and I wonder if just one elephant counts as a stampede.

East of Chincoteague was Piney Island, which as I recall was not really a island but a peinisular. East of Piney Island was Assateague Channel and then come Assateague Island, which was called a shelter island for the way it kept ocean storm waves from tearing up Chincoteague Island. There weren't no bridge to Assateague from Chincoteague like there is today. I would say that little bridge changed the island way of life, letting the city sports drive their automobiles through the town and right over to the beach at Assateague. The inslaught of summer tourists changed Chincoteague from a quaint waterman town to a town full of motels filled with strangers who lines the pockets of Chincoteague merchants ever summer nowadays.

One thing about Chincoteague in nineteen and forty-eight was you could tell pretty well where you was standing just by the smell. My daddy could stick his head out the window and tell you where the wind was blowing from by what he smelt. You can guess what it smelt like in the neighborhood they called Chicken City where probably a couple hundred thousand chickens was being raised all the time. Close to the Beebe Ranch at the South end of the island, the smell was hoss turds, though a lot of folks kept a hoss in their back yard, so the hoss-turd smell was not only at the Beebe Ranch. A nicer smell was the Hooks Bakery on Willow Street. You smelt fresh baked bread for a couple hundred yards lee of it. In the middle of town was the big oyster shucking houses where my daddy opened oysters in the season. There was big piles of oyster shells twenty, thirty foot high all over the place, rotting, stinking, and hatching flies. You sure knowed when you was there.

And that last is where I get my opinion about the Indian meaning of Chincoteague being "Many Smelly Piles of Oyster Shells." It is a fact of history that them Indians et a lot of oysters and left piles of shells all over the place.

When tomaters was ripe, a lot of island women including my mom Leona worked at the tomater canning factory that was built jutting over Chincoteague Channel on pilings. Tomaters was a big crop of farmers on the mainland. My mom and a lot of other women cored tomaters and skinned 'em after the tomaters had been dipped in hot blanching water to loosen the skin. I think they got thirty-five cent an hour. That seems like low wages today, but things was a lot cheaper then. I remember gasoline was sixteen cent a gallon, though not many folks had automobiles, and our house rent was six dollar a month.

Big flatbed trucks brought shiny red vine-ripe tomaters from them farms over on the mainland in peck or bushel baskets all day long to the factory. You could take a couple right off a truck to eat. All us young'uns did that. Nobody minded. I remember how sweet, yet tangy, them sun-warmed ripe tomaters was, how we rinsed 'em in the salt water of Chincoteague Channel to get the yellow dust and sand off of them. And how the juice and seeds squirted on the front of your shirt if you was not careful how you bit.

It was something to watch all that went on to get them tomaters into tin cans. There was a man brung boxes of empty tin cans to a man on a high flatform, who, with each hand, stuck his five fingers in the open ends of five of them tin cans, holding a sixth can in the middle under each palm, them five cans in a circle holding that middle can. That way he plucked twelve of them big cans out of the box at once, six in each hand, and in one motion laid 'em on their sides to roll down a metal chute to land with the open end up on a moving belt front of the women doing the skinning and coring. The women filled the cans, which went in a machine that popped on the tin lid. Then batches of them sealed cans was stacked on a six foot square flatform and lowered into real hot water for a time, then to a machine that pasted a paper label on each can. Then a man put them filled and labeled cans back in the same boxes the empty cans come in, pasted on a label on the box, stacked the boxes on a truck and away they went to the mainland. It was a fascinating thing, the way it just went on and on till the five o'clock steam whistle blowed.

The tomater factory was built on pilings over the water. It is kindly hard to recall exactly where it was, due to subsequent construction along the waterfront, but by my reckoning, it was just North of where the Coast Guard Station is today. All the tomater cores, stems, skins, and spilt juice was dumped directly in Chincoteague Channel. There was always a lot of fish under that factory. Fish was so thick under that factory you could throw a line in the water there with no bait on your hooks and snag a couple Black Wills, as we called small Sea Bass. Lot of bones but sweet eating, them Black Wills. There was all kinds of fish feeding there, but mostly Black Wills. Enviromeddlers on TV today would call it polelution but I think if nowadays we had us a tomater factory dumping their cores and skins in the channel, there'd be lots more fish, instead of self-repointed experts saying it's our fault there's no fish.

Tomater factory blowed up one morning just before all the women was about to start work and that was the end of that. I was in bed and heard it but it did not sound a loud bang, just a whoosh. I thought it was just another rocket test at Wallops Island. After the factory blowed up they closed 'er down, permanent.

One woman walking in the door to get to work early got hurt in the head by a flying brickbat, but the only one died was the man who runned the boiler. Folks said he put cold water into a hot boiler one time too many. He blowed up with it. They found most of him but I expect what parts of him they did not find was the last meal them Black Wills got out of that tomater factory. I did not feel right eating fish for some time after.

Every July the Chincoteague Volunteer Fire Department had a carnival to raise money for fire fighting equipment. They still does that carnival today. There was rides and other amusements for the young'uns, food and bingo for them as liked it, and some things copied from PT Barnum, such as a nickle to see a cow with her tail where her head ought to be. After you paid yer five cent and went in and seen all it was was a cow with her tail in the feed trough, it helped you feel better to wait outside the exit and laugh at the next bunch of suckers when they come out.

Several days before the last Thursday in July, a bunch of Volunteer Firemen with hosses went to the island called Assateague to round up wild ponies that live there. They still does that today, too. I won't try to explain how ponies come to live on Assateague. There's lots of books and theories on that. As I recall, they had not put up the bridge from Chincoteague to Assateague by forty-eight, so the hossmen took their hosses across to Assateague on monitors, which was big flat square scows used in the oyster business. My grandpop built a shack on one of them monitors and anchored it up the bay and the whole family went there during hot spells. Had a coal oil cookstove and beds and everthing a soul needed to live, right there on the water.

As for the Firemen hossmen, one or two of them "salt water cowboys," I believe it was a Baltimore newspaper writer named 'em that, used the occasion for a drinking spree, but they was mostly church men, severely dry.

They took their hosses and camped over to Assateague a few days while doing the round-up, and on the Wednesday before the last Thursday in July, swum them ponies they had rounded up across the channel to Chincoteague, and herded 'em through the streets to pens on the carnival grounds. The next day, Thursday, one of them fast talkers, such as Speedy Riggs who auctioned t'baccer for the American T'baccer Company, auctioned off the colts as kind of a climax to the carnival, though carnival was kept open until the follering Saturday night at eleven-thirty.

They had what you call Blue Laws then, meaning the church-going holy prunes liked to control everybody's Sabbath activities, meaning even the Chincoteague Volunteer Fire Department's Carnival better be shut tight by midnight

Saturday night or them front-pew holy prunes would show 'em who really was in charge on that island. Funny how money changes things. These days you can do just about anything of a Sunday on that island, from drinking spirits to miniature golf now that them front-pew hippocrits makes money on it.

To keep folks coming to carnival them last couple of nights after Pony Penning Day, they ended them two evenings with an act at eleven or eleven-thirty. It was usually what you would call a high wire act. I remember The Seven Plums of the Air, women who climbed a hundred feet up and did tricks swaying side-to-side on limber poles. And they did not wear much. The Plums come back several times year after year. There was rumors that they was somewhat loose with their favors, if you foller me there, and was right tight with the man who hired the acts.

Another act was the man who dived a belly-flop from a great height into a tank filled up with what looked to be three foot of water that had a fire floating on top of it. But I watched him set it up and he dug a hole three foot under the tank so he had six foot of water in that pool. All the same, I would not do it. There was always rumors after the acts packed up and went to the next town that some terrible thing happened. You might hear that the diving man was cut in half on the rim of his tank, for example. Or one of the Plums' pole broke, and she impaled on it. The possibility of such an accident was likely what brung a lot of folks to watch them acts. But I never heard of anything terrible like that happening at our carnival, so I don't put much stock in them stories.

The Pony Penning brought lots of folks to Chincoteague from cities near and far. As I recall it, they was only two hotels, the Channel Bass Hotel on Church Street, and the Russell Hotel, which was across the street from the fishdock, and islanders rented out rooms in their homes to tourists. I believe they still does that today, though these days there is sure a bunch of motels on that island.

The carnival grounds before ninteen and forty-five was not where it is today. In them days, I believe it was across the street from Mumford Street, between Main Street and Chincoteague Channel on the West side of South Main Street. The grounds was much smaller then and had no hoss racing track around it as it did when it was moved futher south on South Main Street, where it still is today.

Colerts did not go on the carnival grounds, except to come to the back of the food stand to buy an oyster samwich, which was a treat lots of folks had to have ever year, and many even come from the mainland to get their oyster samwich. Weren't no law I know of saying colerts could not go on the carnival grounds, they just did not do it. Mostly if they was interested, they watched from the sidewalk across the street. A similar thing, but opposite, happened at the colert's church on the island. I could be wrong but my recollection is that it was called Freewill Methodist Church and it was on Willow Street across from Cleveland Street. It set up high on concrete blocks, I expect in case of real high tides, and though it got whitewashed every spring, it always looked like it needed a fresh coat, though the stain-glass arch-top windows kindly drawed your attention away from the peeling whitewash. That church had a nice big yard all around it, and the mainland colerts parked their cars and a bus on one side of the church so as to leave room for the white folks to sit in the churchyard on the other side. White folk never went inside. The undertaker did stand at the door, passing out free fans with his ad on them to the colerts as they entered but he joined the white folks sitting on the grass outside the church when the preaching and singing commenced. I passed many a hot summer Sunday evening sitting outside there, even joining in on the "amens" and "hallilouyas" when I was moved by the spirit. I don't recall what happened to that old wood church, but there's a motel on that spot on Willow Street now.

At the carnival grounds, in the mornings, we used to look for lost coins. Best pickings was around the slot machine booth. Gambling was against the law but I guess eyes was closed due to the charity nature of the carnival. Or could have been bribes, I don't know. I remember the Sheriff, who I seldom seen outside the County Seat of Accomac except just before elections, was often seen near them slots. But I was never in a position to know, not never being a Fireman. Mostly, watermen did not join the Volunteer Firemen back then, it being hard to answer a fire alarm whistle from three mile up the bay with nothing but an eight-foot sculling oar to fight a three-knot unfavable tide.

Bo Hopkins, the town bum, was always at the carnival grounds looking for coins. He never walked on the sidewalk, always in the dirt in-between the blacktop road and sidewalk, the gutter. Ask him why, he mumble out of the side of his mouth that he did not pay no taxes so sidewalks wasn't his to use. He always talked out the side of his mouth, the other side being used to contain his t'baccer chaw. He weren't too neat with his chaw, often slobbering a dribble down his chin and not being too careful where he let go with his spitting. You could hear him coming because he clicked when he walked, having in his pockets a lot of marbles that he found in the gutter where he walked. He used to sell them marbles for folks to put in the bottom of their goldfish bowls. He wore several pair trousers and several shirts, even in hot weather, and his shoes was always too big for his feet. I saw him stuffing newspaper in the toes one time to make 'em fit better. I don't think he washed much. You could see dirt through the quarter-inch beard on his face and his fingernails had lots of dirt under 'em, they being about an inch long and kindly wild, curling every which way. His eyes was strange too. One eye looked at you and the other eye had a blue cloud over it and looked at his nose. Young'uns used to foller him and tease him, saying, "Git a job, git a job." He never seem to pay 'em no mind, just kept on shuffling and clicking on his way. Folks said he probably had a lot of money hid in that old tarpaper shack he lived in, and when he died, a bunch of people spent the better part of a Saturday tearing that shanty down looking for a trove, even dug up the ground under it but all they found was five shoeboxes full of marbles and some Roosevelt For President politic buttons. Law drove them fools away.

Speaking of the law, there was two police on the island then. Did not seem like there was a lot of crime so two was all that they thought was needed. Their time was spent jailing drunks and an occasional wife-beater, or giving reckless driving tickets to drivers who squealed their tires when turning a corner, that being before what they call low pressure tires come on the scene. Squealing tires back then was an automatic ticket for reckless driving. The chief was named Mitchum, called "Mitch" and the other was "Turk" Turkington. They was tolerant of all us young'uns, 'specially as we was always teasing them, one of us saying, when we knowed they was in earshot, "Get 'im Turk," and the other of us answering, "Got 'im, Mitch." All us children teased 'em like that, and there must a been a good story behind "Get 'im, Turk, Got 'im Mitch," but to this day I do not know what it was.

Carnival was loud. There was steam organ ragtime hurdy-gurdy music ever time the merry-go-round turned, which it seemed like was all the time, and the Ferris Wheel runned off a diesel electric generator that groaned louder when it was put to work, which also it seemed was all the time. And there was records played over loudspeakers, and endless pubic service announcements for the crowd. You could hear the noise all over the island, especially downwind. And folks slept with their windows open, homes having no air conditioning on that island back then. I remember laying in my bed a quarter mile from the carnival, hearing over and over, Earnest Tubb, or could have been Eddy Arnold, singing, "They say a man's home is his castle and he's like a king on a throne. It may be a shack down alongside the tracks but everthing in it's his own." Man who played the records must have liked that tune.

The carnival had something for everybody: A Ferris Wheel for light courting, a tilt-a-whirl for excitement, a merry-go-round for tottlers, hot dog, hamburger, and oyster samwiches, soft drinks, and popcorn for the hongry, Bingo for light gamblers, and for the foolhardy, a Big Six Dice Wheel and slot machines for the foolish. Some folks justifiably called them slots "one-armed bandits". There was yellow lights strung like a ceiling all over the grounds and at the start of carnival the ground was covert with fresh yellow pine chips from the mainland sawmills. Chips looked nice and give off a nice smell.

    Speaking about smells again, when you first come on the toll road on the mainland end, you got a whiff of the sulphur marsh smell, worser if the tide was low. Funny, by the time you got to the Chincoteague end of the toll road, you did not notice that smell no more. Another thing, though there wasn't many flush toilets back then, the hotels had 'em, and their big cesspools had wooden tops that got holes rotten in them quick due to the heavy atmosphere on their undersides. Strolling past a hotel on a real hot day, you might get a breeze once in a while bringing a certain unpleasantness to your nose that caused you not to be sure which was worst, the hot day or the cool breeze."

# Session Three
## (Recorded July 20, 1999)
### Memories

"I hope all the dry stuff I said up to now did not bore you, but I had to get it out of the way. I will now start my memories of the summer of forty-eight. That was the time I spent just about ever day playing with my friends Ben and Lottie Dale. Right here I got to say that Ben and Lottie was colerts. I took a lot a teasing about always being with Ben and Lottie that summer from white folks, some right mean about it, and I expect Ben and Lottie got their share of grief from colerts too, but seemed to me like the nastier people was to us, the closer friends we three young'uns was. Another thing kept us close was we knew we would not see one another very much when the summer was over because of the schools. My school, the school for white children, was on Chincoteague, on Church Street, whereas the colert school was on the mainland over to Wattsville I think, six, seven mile away from Chincoteague. Used to be a colert school on Chincoteague a long time ago, in the twenties, I think, but as the colerts moved away, it wasn't equalnomical so they moved it to the mainland. I could walk to my school, but the colert school was too far for Ben and Lottie to walk, so when school was on they stayed with some of their relations to the mainland near the colert school.

As I remember it, there was only three colert families living on the island in forty-eight, not counting Navy colerts from the base on the mainland. But I don't recall ever seeing a Navy colert on the island. I expect they stayed to the mainland, where the Navy base was located, and where there was things interesting to colert boys, such as dancing, churching, drinking, and above all, a lot a young colert gals.

The Dales was one of them three colert families lived on Chincoteague, and as they lived close by me, they was the family I was most knowledgeable of, and I will fill you in on their details later.

Second colert family lived on the island was Mister Rob and Miss Rhoda Williams. They lived Up the Neck to a place folks called Wildcat. Even though Chincoteague was not a big island, there was a lot of neighborhoods there with names like that. Names like Chicken City, Snotty Ridge, Deep Hole, Eastern Side, and Up the Neck. Mostly them places was named for where they was or what went on there, though there wasn't no remarkably deep hole in Deep Hole that I know of. Chicken City did have hundreds of thousands of fryers being raised there all the time. Later on, in the sixties, a lot of them chicken houses was made into motels when the city swells started coming to the island and simutaneous the chicken business fell off. Nowdays them motels has a lot of nice flowers growing around them, I expect due to the hundreds of layers of chicken droppings fertilizing the area over the years. Another island neighborhood was Snotty Ridge. Though everybody else on Chincoteague called it Snotty Ridge, Snotty Ridgers themselves mostly called their area Rattlesnake Ridge for reasons of pride, and in later years when that area was divided into building lots, they changed the name to just Ridge Road. Getting rid of the rattlesnake part of the name made the lots sell better, I expect. Never was no rattlesnakes on Chincoteague to my mind, just black snakes and in the glades, water moccasins. Folks claim that occasionally a copperhead was brought from the mainland in bales of feed hay for the hosses, but I never saw one and I doubt it. I could not tell you Mister Rob's favor because he was seldom seen in town. He made his living on the water. Like a lot of watermen, he did not spend a lot of time in town or do much socializing. Mister Rob's wife Miss Rhoda looked like one a them Aunt Jermimers, fat and always with an apron on and a red bandanner on her head, except when she went to church. Then she was rigged out in clothes make any white woman jealous. For a living, she did different things like wall-paper for people or mind their young'uns or work in the tomato canning factory. I heard tell she also sold moonshine out their back door. A lot of folks, colert and white, brewed up a little lightning or applejack and sold what little they did not need for personal consuming.

Third colert family weren't exactly a family, just a woman named Puddy Boggs, a pretty woman always dressed in six inch spike heel shoes and flashy red or black dresses, some with slits up to her stern, and her with no pettycoat, giving full view of her black net silk stockings and red lacy garters in that slit, often also wearing a black pillbox hat with a red net veil, all the time looking at her face in a compac mirror, powdering her nose, painting on a fresh set of red lips or tongueing a little spit on the tip of her little finger and smoothing her eyebrows with it. She smelt good, too. I seen her buy Evening in Paris perfume at the Ben Franklin store. Miss Puddy lived in a nice apartment in the middle of town over the bowling alley, which when the Navy Base cut down on personnel after the war, went belly up and closed and a Russian feller, some said he was a spy but the whole US country was spy shy after the war, opened Hanley's Restaurant there, which was across the street from an ice cream parlor. Miss Puddy's apartment was convenient to where Tim and Shorty parked their taxicabs. Fifty cent to go anywhere on the island, a dollar to go to the Navy Base. She did not have no regular job but had a lot of men visitors, both sailor boys from the navy base and permanent island men, who gave her gifts, if you understand what I'm getting to there.

There was one more colert I want to tell you about though he did not live on the island. I believe his proper name was Jim Baine but folks called him Crackerdust. He drove a rusty-fender, cracked windshield, old thirty-four Ford flatbed truck with no taillights, just reflectors, and with fifty-five gallon oak-staved barrels and a galvanized steel table and an A-frame and ropes and block and tackles all piled up on it looking like it might all fall off if he hit a substantial bump in the road. A lot of folks on Chincoteague raised hogs in their back yards then. Hogs et just about anything you put in their trough, apple cores, corncobs, fat meat, tater peelings, in short, just about all the food wastes you might have to take to the garbage dump today. Such wastes was called slops. I guess that's why feeding hogs was called slopping 'em. Crackerdust made his living in late fall and early winter, butchering them hogs. He would bury a fifty-five gallon oak-stave barrel set at a forty-five degree angle so they could dip slaughtered hogs in lye to remove their hair. Then he set up his galvanized butcher table with a hand meat grinder at one end and a sausage stuffer, too. There was always several women around the table, each ready to do their job, be it making sausage, souse, or whatever else the hog owner wanted from that hog. To us young'uns it was something like setting a stage for a play and when Crackerdust decided everthing and everybody was ready he would hoist a hog up that A-frame by the hind legs. Then, like he is the star of the stage show, he put on his white oilcloth butcher's apron, then slowly squirt a shot of Three-In-One oil on a whetstone and careful put a fresh edge on an eighteen-inch butcher knife, all the while that pig screaming so loud it hurt your eardrums. Then Crackerdust grab that hog's ear and slice its throat, and while the hog kicking his last, blood pouring into a washtub to save for sausages, Crackerdust always look us young'uns in the eye while grinning his toothless grin, stick out his long purple tongue and slow lick the hot, steaming blood offen that butcher knife. We always knew it was coming and it scared us terrible, but something made us have to watch it. And a show like that is awful hard to forget. I tell you about him so later if I tell you some momma or pappa tells a young'un to "Behave or I will sic Crackerdust on you," you will understand why us young'uns might tend to behave ourselfs.

My friends Ben and Lottie was the only colert young'uns on the island. They was twins. Did not look identical nor even much favor one another, just born on the same day. We was all three of us the same age, twelve. They was kindly light-complected, and both had a few freckles on their cheeks, but their momma and daddy was right dark colorerts, and had no freckles as I recall. Ben was a couple inches taller'n me and Lottie was about tall as me. Ben's hair was real short and he had one of them fake parts in his hair that a lot of colert men has. I never asked him about it but I always wondered how they got that line in there. Lottie's kinky hair was black, but when the sun hit it, you saw a reddish-orange tinge to it. It was always braided up in pigtails out of each side of her head and crossed over the top ear-to-ear, kindly like a handle with a yellow ribbon at each end up there. She had big brown eyes look like a deer's and the longest eyelashes I ever saw.

I knew the Dale young'uns better than just about anybody because they lived almost in my back yard and we been playing together from time to time from my youngest memories. I lived on the east side of South Main Street and Ben and Lottie lived in a cinder-block bungalow in the pine woods in back of my house, between South Main Street and Willow Street, which did in fact have a lot of Willow trees along it in people's front yards. The Dale house was about fifty or seventy-five yard back of my house. There was woods all down the middle of Chincoteague back then, and there was water in them woods from one end of the island to t'other. They called it a canal. It went north-south down the middle of the island. Not a real canal, only a lot of ponds and glades more or less connected, full of cat-tails. I know it was fresh water in it 'cause it froze once in a while and we ice-skated in it. I had a pair of ice skates that clamped on the soles of your regular shoes. Not too hot for skating but considering we only got 3 or 4 days ice skating in a year, they did the job for me. Lotta folks trapped muskrat in them glades and sold the fur pelts to Sears Roebuck. A lot of folks et muskrat, too. My grandpop loved it but just the sight of it, laying there cooked brown on a serving platter, slit open belly full of dumplings or taters and greens, grinning up at me kindly upset me. It smelt real gamey too. Good muskrat pelt brought sixty-five, seventy cent, I recall. You used to see houses with a rack of pelts leaning up on the side, fur side in, stretched and drying in the sun.

Another thing about my friend Lottie was she start ever sentence she ever said with, "Gracious", and if she got excited she start it with "Gracious, gracious," and the more excited she got, the more graciouses come out of her, long strings of 'em sometimes.

In them days most young'uns except them with snooty mommas went barefooted soon as warm weather come. Our mommas did not mind as it was equalnomical not having no shoes wearing out and no socks to wash. Took a while for your feet to get tough, so first part of summer you stepped more careful than later on, and you did not walk down no oyster-shell rutty roads if you did not have to, on account of you might cut your tender feet. Lowest rank in the Boy Scouts is Tenderfoot. Must be a connection there somewheres.

Weren't no road to Ben and Lottie's house from South Main Street, just a winding footpath of tromped-down brown pine needles, we called 'em shats, through them pines and across a little dried-up glade back of my yard. There was a crushed oyster-shell rutty road to their house from Willow Street, but mostly folks took a short cut through our yard and went through them pines.

The Dale's house was right nice far as colert's houses go, and Ben's daddy owned it outright, whereas my daddy's house was bigger but it was rented. All three of them colert families on the island had nice living arrangements. Fact is, they was a leg up on many mainland colerts far as acomudations was concerned, many mainland colerts living in labor camp housing or in the most run down houses there was. That don't mean they all was living in hovels. There was also considerable colerts in real nice houses on the mainland, but overall, I had to say Chincoteague colerts was a cut above the mainland variety far as living arrangements went.

Folks called Ben's daddy "Big Ben" and called little Ben "Ben-Boy" so's you would know which of them they was cussing or discussing. A lot of folks had names like that for the same reason. There was Bobby John Disney and Bobby Lee Disney, Joe Tim Reid and Joe Boy Reid, and many more, some being father and sons, and some, no relation at all, just happening to have the exact same name due to coincidence, there being a lot of families with the same last name on that island. Some folks called Big Ben Nigger Ben, but not to his face. To his face he was called Mister Ben, like any other colert. Seemed like to me the lowest white folks made themself feel bigger by always referencing colerts as Niggers. I don't think most of them actually hated colerts but they did take just about any opportunity to degrade 'em. High class folks did it once in a while, too. Hell, I even done it sometimes. Could not hardly not do it when everybody round you doing it.

Big Ben had a good job in the Virginia Civil Service, making him better off than three-quarters of the unhabitants of Chincoteague Island. He worked in the state package store. I never understood why they call it a package store, it sold liquor. It's right interesting how he come to work there. The three white clerks did not feel right serving colerts, and colerts was right steady customers of that business, the nearest other liquor store being some miles away, across the Maryland state line, or down the peninsular to Onancock, so the state hired Big Ben to handle serving the colert customers, thus sparing the two white clerks their embarrasment. Big Ben could also serve white customers, that apparently being acceptable to all concerned.

My daddy admired Big Ben. Daddy always said Big Ben had a wage rain or shine and did not have to get mud on his hands like a watermen to earn it. And he would get a good pension from the state and not end up in the poorhouse like some. All the same, I imagine Big Ben done more than an equal share of work in that store, him being the only colert, and the only one there who would wait on all customers. Lots of white folks was jealous of Big Ben because of that good job which they themselves would not take because they felt it was below them to serve colerts. That's what you might say is a paradox.

When you took that path of shats through the pine woods and across the glade from my back yard to Ben's house, you ended up right to Ben's front yard, if you could call it a yard. First thing struck your eye was that the whole yard was covert by a woodpile shape like a Egypt pyramid, high as the eaves of their roof. The wood most used for home stoves in forty-eight was lumbermill trimmings. The mainland back then was covert with yellow pine with an occasional farmer's open field. Had so many stands of them yellow pines that the state put up fire watch towers manned with fire wardens ever so many miles, cause nothing burns like dry pine trees. Nowdays there's not much of them yellow pines left. Most of it was chopped down, and what land that was replanted was sowed with Loblolly Pines, which looks similar but grows much faster. Anyway, each piece of that firewood had a straight saw-cut side and a rounded side covert with bark. It was what was left over when they cut a square piece of lumber out the center of a pine log. The Dale's woodpile shrunk over the winter as it was burned in their stoves to heat the house and cook.

My yard did not have no woodpile. My daddy had switched to coal for heat and cooking though most Chincoteague folks still used wood. Coal was neater. You carried coal in a scuttle, lots neater than carrying an armload of wood, no splinters snagging your sweater, no bark all over the floor We kept ourn in a coal bin in a shed back of our kitchen. And that shed was kindly a hideout for me, where I built lots of models of airplanes like I saw at the Navy base, out of soft balser wood. Coal was cleaner burning than pine trimmings, too, and safter. I mean hard coal, called Anthrucite. There was lots less chimley fires from burning coal on account of coal has no sap. In school they told us coal burns longer because it denster than wood. Just think how oak burns longer than pine. That is 'cause it's a little denster. Coal a hundred times denster than oak. Fascinating thing.

That woodpile in the Dale's front yard made it near impossible to get to their front door without climbing over some wood. Just as well, because nobody come to nobody's front door in them days anyhow except preachers and insurance salesmen and some folks did not mind if the struggle to get to their front door caused preachers or insurance salesmen to eliminate their next visit.

On TV today, there's lots of enviromeddlers talking about polelution. Well, you ain't never seen no polelution until you seen all them Chincoteague chimleys pouring smoke up in the air. Sometimes when the atmosphere was just right, smoke would come out a chimley and flow down the outside of that chimley to the ground and spread out and then you did not have to smoke no cigarette to inhale smoke. It was kindly like what they call smog in Californey, I think. On the other side of that, I seen nights so crispy clear there was a band of stars across the sky you thought you could reach out and pluck one for yourself.

Off to one side of Ben's back yard was their water well. My daddy's house had town water, with two spikets, one outside in the back yard and one in the kitchen. The outside one was right handy for rinsing off your feet so's not to track up your kitchen linoldium floor. No hot water though. If you needed hot water, say to take a all-over bath of a Saturday, you heated a basin full of water on the kitchen stove, set it on the kitchen table oilcloth and took a washcloth bath right there in the kitchen. Did not have water meters then, I believe it was a straight fifty cent ever three months no matter how much water you used.

My daddy's house had a gas line to it with a meter too, but we did not use it. You put a quarter in a slit and it give you so much gas for cooking. Gas man come around with a key and open the coin box ever now and then, but he stopped coming to our house. My daddy said he would not use it because you might be in the middle of cooking a Sunday dinner when the gas run out and you with no quarters and Charlie Gail's general store up the street closed because of the Blue Laws so you could not get no change, in which case you would have to fire up the coal range anyway, so why not use the coal range to begin with.

In ninteen and forty-eight, there was a lot of water wells like the Dales had in their yard. Not picture book round wells with stone walls and a crank-up bucket hanging on a rope like you might see on a framed sampler on somebody's living room wall. Chincoteague wells was just galvanized pipe drove deep in the ground with a pump handle screwed on top of it. I remember how that pump water was sweet, which struck me odd because if you dug down six foot, all you got was salt water, but go down fifty, sixty foot, and you got sweet drinking water. With all the houses and motels built on Chincoteague since then, adding I can't guess how many cesspools, I wonder if the water would be fit to drink, let alone sweet tasting.

Another thing about them wells was there was always a Mason jar of water next to them. If you wanted water from the well, you had to pour some of that water from the Mason jar into the top of the pump. They called that priming the pump. If you did not do that you would jack that pump handle up and down all day without no water coming. When you finished getting your drink of water, you had to be sure to leave the Mason jar filled with water so the next feller could prime the pump. Some folks did not want just anybody drinking out of their pump, so they would take their jar of priming water in their house with them. All the drinking water to Chincoteague nowadays comes through big pipes alongside the toll road from wells over to the mainland.

At the back of Ben's back yard was their one-hole privy. My daddy's house had a privy too, but it was a three-holer, two for grownups and one a little lower and smaller round for young'uns, each hole with a lid having hinges made out of old shoe leather. There wasn't many folks had inside toilets then, and there's hardly no outdoor privies now, so if you will excuse me for describing such a delicate act, I better discuss the way you did your toilet business back then. Our privy was about twenty foot back of our coal shed and its door faced the pine woods. If it weren't raining or windy or otherwise unclement, you might unhook the screen door spring that usually automatic closed the door. Then you might prop the door open with the cinder-block left there for that use, and close the two lids on the other two holes on account of the smell, and you might occupy your mind observing them pine woods and wildlife, making your daily chore right pleasurable.

For toilet paper folks used last year's Sears & Roebuck, Montgomery Ward, or sometimes other catalogs. There was one catalog out of Chicago that besides the normal items like the other two catalogs had, carried a lot of flashy colert clothes, styles like zoot suits, trousers with watch chains hanging to the knees and porkpie hats with brims so wide you could use them for an umbreller. For a joke, folks called the catalogs Sears and Sawbuck or Monkey Ward. I never got that joke.

First catalog paper you used as toilet paper for wiping was the yellow index pages where you looked up what page a catalog item was on. Them yellow pages was thinner and easier on your stern. Catalog companies did not send you next year's catalog unless you order something this year, and I don't know how folks in that situation did their wiping 'cause I don't remember seeing rolled-up toilet paper in stores then. Couple other things about them toilets: First thing, you had to give the whole area a right thorough inspection for spiders before you set down. Spiders seem to love privies, and though there weren't much danger from spiders in general, there was the occasional Black Widder, real or imagined. Second thing was that you passed a lot a time looking at different items in them catalogs and I expect a lot of folks catalog orders was first thought about in privies. And one last thing I got to mention is the color photographs in the women's foundation garment and underwear pages. Them pictures got a lot of intense study by boys like me entering their manly age."

# Session Four
## (Recorded July 27, 1999)
### Sky King

"Machine running? The only real hero I ever had other than my daddy was my Uncle Walt. I always thought Uncle Walt looked like Smilin' Jack in the funny papers. He was slender and had the same moustache and slicked-back black hair and was right strongly in demand by the island and mainland girls. He could not read nor write when he got drafted to war in the Navy but they got him his high school diploma and give him a real chance at a good life. After the war, the government gave ever veteran school money called the GI Bill. Many folks did not want to go to college or learn a trade, but they did want to use the money the government give them, which had to be spent on education. So up sprung a lot of flying schools, which qualified to have that money spent on them. My uncle Walt took to flying and after he got his private pilot license, he went on and got his commercial and instructor licenses also, and he become the instructor at the flying school on Chincoteague, which used float-planes, land being in short supply. There was a Taylorcraft, we called it a Tee-cart, an Aeronca, we called it the Airnocker, and a Piper Cub, just called a Cub. All of them was kindly minimal airplanes that Leo Samage, the owner of the flying school, had picked up cheap from war surplus with 50 or 65 horsepower engines. Later on, the school got a Stinson Station Wagon which had a Franklin engine. We called that one the Wagon. That one was a land plane, no pontoons. They did set up a bumpy 1000 foot landing strip in the marsh south of the Beebe Ranch for a while. Because of the lay of the land, they set it up more or less North-South, making for interesting crosswind landings and takeoffs as the wind almost always come at that strip sideways. They also had an amphibian Republic SeaBee which was like a flying boat with wheels you could crank down to land on land. The SeaBee had a pusher propeller and also had a Franklin engine. I don't recall the horsepower but it was a lot more than the other airplanes had. It was a four-seater as was the Wagon, whereas the other three airplanes was two-seaters. Leo Samage got a contract with the goverment to deliver mail and other papers from Washington down the coast to all the Coast Guard Lifesaving stations as far as Okracoke Island in Carolina, and Lee and Uncle Walt took turns doing that mail run. They had the back seats removed out of that SeaBee to make room for the bags of correspondence they was hauling to the stations. I went with Uncle Walt on a few occasions and I will say more about that later.

Me and Ben hung around the seaplane base quite a lot. Lottie wasn't interested so she stayed away. At the end of the day, or when no more flights was scheduled, the float-planes was water-taxied fast enough so they would slide right up a wood ramp which was coated with axle-grease. Then we pulled the airplanes sideways across the greased dock until there was three airplanes sitting on that dock and then the SeaBee with its wheels cranked down was taxied up on the shore. Had to be right careful how you stepped around that dock 'cause that axle grease was real slick and more than once I was arse over tin cup doing that job. When the planes was all up on the dock us young'uns washed the salt water off of the airplanes and tied 'em down for the night. We got no pay for this, but often got to ride with Uncle Walt or one of the other instructors and get unofficial flying instruction. After a while, Uncle Walt let us boys do the taxiing and parking of them airplanes, and for that alone, we was the envy of most of the other boys on Chincoteague. One calm evening after many days of doing the taxiing job without incident and having done quite a bit of flying with Uncle Walt, I had put up the Airnocker, Ben wasn't there that day, and I had also put up the Cub, and was about to wade out to get the Tee-cart when Uncle Walt says, "You're pretty good at taxiing. Think you could fly it?"

I did not hesitate. "Damn right!" I had got in the ungentlemanly habit of punctuating my language with a cussword ever now and then to give me a kindly adult sound.

"Well, you go ahead and take her around the pond one time. Remember everthing I have taught you and if you think there is any chance at all that you will not do an absolutely perfect landing, why you go around and line 'er up and try again."

My heart was pounding as I stepped up out of the waist-high water onto the Tee-Cart's pontoon and opened the door, leaned inside and cracked the throttle, gave 'er a half a shot of prime, and switched both magneto switches to "on". Then I untied the plane from its mooring buoy and unclipped the paddle from the side of the pontoon and paddled the plane so it pointed away from the mooring buoy towards the open water. I stowed the paddle and stepped in front of the wing struts. I held onto the strut behind me and flipped the wood propeller from behind as I had done many times with Uncle Walt at the controls. Uncle Walt even did it three thousand feet up in the Cub once when we were doing stalls and the engine died and the prop stopped windmilling. He just climbed out on the pontoon and said, "Hold her level and in of sixty mile per hour glide", which I did and it took all the left stick to do it, Uncle Walt's weight out on that right pontoon required it. I thought it a little unusual that he did not just dead-stick land 'er on Tom's Cove which was right below us and he could start her once we got down, but I must tell you, and you will hear later that he was a daredevil at heart. Once when we watched a movie about barnstormers, he kept saying he could do wingwalking good as the movie stuntman we was watching in the movie. Back to my story. The Tee-Cart's sixty-five hoss Continental that I hand-propped started right up and idled nicely as I retraced my way back to the open door and climbed in and scooted over to the pilot's seat past the big round automobile steering wheels that the Tee-cart used for control columns, and I buckled my seatbelt. Then I fast-taxied around in a big circle to put a little ripple on the glassy water. The pontoons would not break free of the water's suction if it was too smooth. There was no wind so I pointed the nose in a direction that would give me the longest runway and fed her the throttle nice and slow and smooth and she got up on the step right away, due to my light weight I expect, and I let her build up to where the airspeed read forty-five or fifty miles per hour and I raised the nose and she leaped into the air. I dropped the throttle back to nineteen hundred and fifty RPM and looked to be sure my oil pressure was OK and it was. I can't tell you how great I felt at that moment. Time slows down at exciting times like this, and I was squeezing ever moment for the enjoyment of it. The adventure was, of course totally illegal. Even back then, you had to be sixteen years of age to legally solo an airplane, but here I was, twelve years old, doing it. I circled the area, using the wing strut parallel to the ground as a safe turning aid, and I was careful to keep the ball centered with the rudder and ailerons coordinated, as I did not want to do a stall by accident. I only climbed up to five hundred feet and did my tour around the pond at that altitude. Then I set up my landing in the opposite direction of my takeoff so as to be able to taxi straight to the greasy ramp. I have to say my landing was a beauty and I cut off the engine just as I approached the ramp, and she slid up onto it, perfect. I dismounted and looked around to see if anybody saw me but even Uncle Walt was nowhere in sight. Seemed like a shame for such a momentous event not to be admired by somebody. I tied the Tee-cart down, rinsed her off, and went into the office shack. Uncle Walt was sitting with his feet on the desk smoking a cigarette.

"How did it go?", he asked me.

"Pretty good," I says.

And he says, "Promise me not to tell anybody. I could get in bad trouble with the CAA for letting you do that."

"I promise." Said I, and I never told another soul about that little adventure until I told you today. I figger Uncle Walt won't mind, He's long dead, rest his soul.

I told you I got drawed down on with a twelve gauge for stealing clams from Charlie Davis's clam bed. Well Uncle Walt was not above picking up a few oysters off of somebody's remote tump. Once I was with him when he suddenly got a urge to get some oysters and he landed the Cub in between two rows of oysters. Oysters was usually planted by shoveling shells off of both sides of a monitor that was being towed, and that made oyster beds be in rows. Anyway, we landed and Uncle Walt pulls two gunny sacks out of the little baggage hole behind the back seat of the Cub and we both start picking up oysters until we had them sacks pretty full. Uncle Walt tied one sack onto the top of each pontoon. Then when we got the two of us in the airplane, the pontoons was hitting the bottom, so Uncle Walt tells me to get out and wait and he'll be right back. Subtracting my weight made the Cub float, and away he flew. I looked around to see if there was a way I could walk and wade to dry land, but the very thing that made this particular tump attractive for thieving, made it a difficult one to walk from, so there I stood. I begun to worry when, I expect it was two hours or more later, the tide had started in and the water was lapping at my knees and the sun getting somewhat low in the West and no sign of Uncle Walt. I was just getting really nervous when I heard the drone of the Cub, and I did not let Uncle Walt see the tear I brushed out of my eye as I scrambled into the Cub for the rescue ride home.

Once in a while my momma and daddy would let me stay overnight with Uncle Walt in his little two-room apartment over a chicken house on Chicken City Road. Judging by their playful mood when I was going to stay with Uncle Walt, I expect them occasions was used by my parents for what I call practicing making babies, but I do not know that for a fact. On the occasions I stayed with Uncle Walt, I got to go with him to deliver the mail to the Coast Guard Stations in the Sea Bee. We would get up at two in the morning and take off from Chincoteague in the SeaBee to arrive in Washington about an hour and fifteen minutes later, around four in the morning. A Coast Guard truck would unload eight or nine locked canvas mail bags and Uncle Walt and I would tie 'em snug in the back of the plane, and we would take off around five, headed east to the Atlantic shore and south there till we got to one of our stops. Uncle Walt would buzz the Coast Guard station and at the same time decide if we could land on the beach or if a water landing seemed preferable, and we would land on one or the other, give the Coast Guard a bag, take a bag from them, and continue to the next stop where the same thing transpired. I noted Uncle Walt had a little commerce going on with them Coast Guard boys. He had a footlocker back under the mailbags and he had a little liquor supply there. Cheap stuff, mostly. Three Feathers, Four Roses. Once I asked him about it and he said, "Don't tell anybody, promise." And I promised and I never did tell anybody until I am telling you now. I guess Uncle Walt was buying liquor at the package store and selling it to them lonely Coast Guard boys. I think regulations did not allow them boys to have liquor on the station. Anyhow, the important thing to remember for this story is we either landed on the water at a station or we cranked down the wheels and landed on the beach.

My Uncle Walt was a busy man with the girls, and it often took a heavy toll on his alertness. On the first few Coast Guard flights, he would get us in the air, up to altitude, point the airplane in the direction of the next stop, trim the airplane for level flight, and say to me, "Keep 'er on this heading. Wake me in fifteen minutes or if something happens." At first I would do it as he said, but as I got better at controlling the airplane, I would just navigate us to the next station and wake him up so he could land the airplane. And that was something that eventually caused a problem.

We took off from Assateague Station one morning where we had landed on the sandy beach and we headed South to our next stop. Uncle Walt was real tired, having not slept the night before due to a hot date with a lady friend, and he just got the airplane off of the beach and said to me, "You got 'er. Take 'er up to five hundred foot and foller the beach to Smith Island Station and wake me when we get there. The airplane felt kindly sluggish to me but I got her lined up as best I could and we flew kindly slow, I thought. Like she was too heavy, but I just kept attending to my pilot duties till we got over the Smith Island Station, when I woke Uncle Walt and he took the controls and came in for a landing on the water. Just before the airplane touched the water, Uncle Walt hollered, "Shit!" and give 'er full rpm and commenced trying to get the landing gear up, which it now occurred to me was why she had been flying so sluggish on me. The landing gear had been sticking down in the wind, causing extra drag. Well, Uncle Walt was not able to get the gear up fast enough and the airplane wheels dug into the water and flipped us upside down. Next thing I know, I am hanging upside down and the engine is screaming a blue note. I saw Uncle Walt flip the mag switches off and it got real quiet real quick except for the steady stream of cusswords coming out of my Uncle Walt. He got himself out of his seatbelt and fell to the roof of the cockpit, stood up and undid my belt and caught me as I fell out of my seat. Then we went out and stood on the wing underside as the SeaBee floated upside down until a Coast Guard rescue boat come out and towed the SeaBee upside down to shore with us on the wing. Then Uncle Walt supervised as they turned the airplane right side up by digging a hole under the nose and winching the tail up and over. Unlike today when the goverment has its nose in ever little thing, no goverment man come around to investigate. I recall the CAA man classified the accident as a "water taxiing incident" and that airplane was fixed and back in service within a month. My Uncle Walt was a little fearful of the fact that he had a locker full of whiskey in the plane, so he used it to pay the Coast Guard boys for their help in righting the airplane and to buy their silence. On the way home in the Stinson, which had been sent to pick us up after the Coast Guard boys telephoned the flying school, Uncle Walt whispered to me, "Don't you ever tell anybody about my sleeping on these runs, and that goes for the whiskey, too." And I never did tell nobody, until now.

    Third thing that happened with Uncle Walt did not happen with me along, but it did affect his flying career. He was up in the Cub one day and happened to find his self flying alongside a vee formation of geese, flying south for the winter. He got to thinking that the hotels paid right good money for fresh goose, and he was pretty sure they did not ask where it come from 'cause folks said hotels was always buying duck and goose from poachers, so after that Uncle Walt took to carrying a shotgun along with him on his flights and one day he again found his self among a bunch of them geese, and he opened the doors of the Cub and was shooting 'em point blank and after he got five or six, swooped down and landed on the water and plucked up the dead geese. Unbeknownst to Uncle Walt, the Game Warden, Herb Brackalew was watching the whole shooting match from below and in them days airplanes had their numbers on the underside of the wings in three foot tall letters, so Brackalew was waiting at the flying school office and when the Cub taxied up, Brackalew arrested Uncle Walt and took him to the courthouse in Norfolk, where Uncle Walt was given a suspended sentence due to his service in the recent war and due to having no past instances of getting caught.

But the CAA took away Uncle Walt's licenses to fly and he finished his days as a bus driver, first for Trailways, then Greyhound, then as a City Bus driver up to Baltimore. The pay wasn't much different, but when I saw Uncle Walt after his goose-hunting incident, he seemed to have lost all his swagger. And the end of Uncle Walt's flying career ended my flying opportunities, too."

# Session Five
## (Recorded August 3, 1999)
### Churches and Baseball

"I'm ready sir, you recording? For a small town, there was lots for us young'uns to occupy ourselfs with, and not too much trouble a young'un could get into. I told you how white folks used to spend hot summer evenings outside of the Freewill Methodist Church. Well, me and my friends Lottie and Ben was entertained by observing a lots of goings-on on that island, but one of our favorites was church activities. Ben and Lottie was right religious and their Sundays and even some other days was took up with church services, but sometimes their folks was off to a camp meeting or left Ben and Lottie home while they went to services to the mainland, their automobile being filled up with the other colerts from the island. I should add that Big Ben's automobile was what they called a "Salesman's Special." I don't remember the brand, but it was a two-door coupe and it come with no back seat, but Big Ben had put in a back seat from a junk car. It did not fit too good but it give them the ability to carry a couple of cramped-up passengers along and it was removable if Mister Ben wanted to haul something. Anyway, I remember one Sunday afternoon that Ben and Lottie come to my back door and, in their quiet voices, asked if anybody was home.

"I'm here in the coal shed," says I, "Let me finish glueing this wing rib and I will be right with you." I held the rib in it's place on the balsa spar until the Testors Model Airplane Cement set up and joined Ben and Lottie on my porch swing where we swung while we talked.

"Gracious, what can we do on a Sunday afternoon?"

"I don't have no plans but to work on my Comet Model of the Hellcat airplane," I says.

"Gracious, my mother says the white folk's Baptist Church is going to have a Baptism ceremony down to the canal. Perhaps we could go watch it."

I need to explain my view of the pecking order of the various religions on the island, having observed them all. The upper class was the Methodists. You could tell even just by looking at their church. Solid. Stone walls. Slate roof. Lots of varnished wood inside. I went to their summer bible school one year and that was where I got interested in building them model airplanes. They were different from Baptists, I'm meaning regular Baptists here, as opposed to your Holy Rollers. A Methodist baptism was symbolic. Preacher just splashed some water in your face, so you will understand later that we young'uns did not spend our time observing Methodists do baptisms. No fun watching a preacher sprinkle somebody with a few drops of water. But the Baptists baptised by total immersion, an altogether interesting sight for reasons I will explain in a minute, so us young'uns got our bicycles and headed off to the place they called "The Canal" at the south tip of the island. Pretty soon we was off the blacktop road of South Main Street onto a rutty oyster shell road that led the last mile to the Canal, and we saw the church bus and a couple of tents and a small crowd on the shore. We laid our bikes in some bullrushes off the road and walked kindly carefully because of the oyster shells, to a dune off to one side of the action where we had an unobstructed view of the proceedings.

The fat preacher, come to think of it I never saw a thin Baptist preacher, he was standing thigh-deep in the water, dressed in his suit coat, white shirt, and tie, but with old pants on. He held in his hand a black leather-cover bible with gold-edged pages and he was preaching a pretty good sermon right there in the water. Then out of one of the two tents come a line of men and out of the other tent come a line of women and girls. The men was dressed in white pants and white shirts and women was dressed in flimsy white cotton feed-sack dresses and they all formed a line from the shore to the preacher and he hands the bible to his wife who was there in the water with him and he shouts at the heavens, "In the name of the Father, the Son, and the Holy Ghost, I baptise you." Or words to that effect. And the baptisee holds his or her nose and the preacher throws 'em backwards under the water and holds 'em there for a count of three, then up they come, some coughing and spitting water, but all starry-eyed, into getting the spirit, and shaking hands and hugging the people on shore, then back to the tent, where they change out of that now clingy feedsack dress. And right there is what attracted us young'uns to watch. You could see practically everthing they had! Clams and wilks of all description. A sex education banquet! Some of the older women wore their foundation garments under their feedsack dresses, but I guess that was frowned on, and I think I learned more about manly and womernly parts from watching Baptist baptisms that from just about anything else.

I must mention here a couple of other similar experiences: I spent a few Sundays at the hardcore church, we called them "Holy Rollers". I watched 'em get the spirit and talk in tongues. Jibberish, mostly, I think, because I did note that there was not a lot of originality in what they said in tongues. Actually they all sounded very much alike. The interesting thing to me was when the would fall on the floor and kick and scream. It was kindly hypnotically amusing to a young'un like me.

The other church I went to once in a while was the Christ Sanctified church. The fun thing there for us young'uns was what they called, "shouting". They all jumped up and down when they sung the Lord's praises, and fifty or so people all hitting the floor simultanishly required them to do special construction on their floors so they would not collapse.

I guess you could go to church ever night of the week if you wanted to. But I prefered the movies. The Pawell Theater charged ten cent on Saturday night and it was usually a western. Gene Autry, Roy Rogers, different young'uns had different favorites. My friend Billy Didrickson loved Sunset Carson, I recall, but my favorite was Lash LaRue. I had my picture took with him when he come to town for a stage show once, along with Fuzzy McNight, one of his sidekicks. Last I heard, old Lash had got religion and was an evangelist in Florida.

The Pawell Theater was the only one in town for many years, but it later become commonly known as the "old" theater when the Island Theater opened. Island Theater was modern. No balcony like the old theater. No westerns. Well, fewer westerns, anyway. It charged more but the pictures was better and soon the old theater was in trouble, so the Pawells opened a new theater called the "New Theater." For a couple of years gave the Island Theater some competition, but eventually both the Pawell Theaters closed, leaving the Island Theater, which become the Roxy Theater when it was bought by a TV star from New Jersey who used Chincoteague as a hideaway.

That about covers churches and movie houses. Now baseball. Us boys decided to have ourselves a baseball team. We was hanging around with a couple of "Fresh Air Kids" from Philadelphia. They was kids from poor families who was sent out to country places like Chincoteague to keep them out of gangs, I think. They were sponsored by local civic clubs like Kiwanis and Elks. But even with Fresh Air Kids, there weren't enough white boys interested enough to make up a nine-man team, so Ben was invited to be the ninth man, and he right quickly become our best player, hitting and fielding well, and consistently. He was looking to be good as his hero, Jackie Robinson, the first major leaguer colert player. All Ben's heroes was colerts. Another one was Joe Louis, the heavyweight boxing champ. Sometimes him and me would box with my friend Bobby's boxing gloves and Ben always took the part of Joe Louis and I took the part of Billy Conn, who was a light-heavyweight boxer who seemed to be the only likely boxer at the time who might have a chance to take the title from Joe Louis. He almost did, but Lewis whipped him and went on to be the longest title-holder in the history of boxing.

In baseball we did not play no permanent positions, just decided among us just before we played, who would be best at what position. Usually we put a tall left hander at first base. Tall so's he could get the high hits down the first base line and a southpaw so he did not have to twist around to throw to second, third, or home base. We spent a lot a time practicing at the baseball diamond back of the high school on Church Street, practicing among ourselves as there wasn't enough boys on that island interested enough to form a second team. Lottie was our umpire, and she did a good job at that, memorizing all the rules and giving unassailable arguments for her decisions. We also spent a lot of time arguing about and trying on different names for our team, finally deciding just in time for our first and only real game, which I will describe later, that our team would be called the Blue Jays.

We did not have much equipment, most of our bats was broke, held together with black electrical tape, what we called tar tape, and our baseballs always had at least a couple of busted stitches making for wicked curve ball pitches and also making it not unusual for a ball's cover to come completely off if you hit it solid, the cover going one direction and insides going another, somewhat confusing the fielders. My momma did buy me a nice mitt for $4.99 from Sears & Sawbuck, a Pee Wee Reese model, which I spent many hours treating with neat's-foot oil to get a good pocket in it. We had no protective pads or catcher's mask, so the position of catcher was the least sought after, partly due to a fowl tip that right early in one of our first practices hit our catcher, which that day was me, under the chin. That would not have been too bad but I had then and still today have the habit of putting my tongue between my teeth when concentrating. I bled a terrible mess when that baseball caused my teeth to nearly bite off my tongue. Just about scared everybody away from that position for the season. I thought serious about going to old Doc LeKintes but the thought of him sewing stitches in my tongue was more powerful than the pain I had now that most of the bleeding was stopped, so I just laid down in the grass and tried to think up my story to tell my mom so she wouldn't cut me off of baseball.

Doc LeKintes was kindly an interesting experience, so I will interrumpt here to tell you how doctoring was then. It was, I think, two dollar for an office visit, or three dollar for a home visit, a considerable amount for somebody making 35 or 40 cent an hour. Nobody did not have no health insurance, so you did not run to a doctor with ever little thing, or even some right serious things if you was poor. Doc LeKintes's office was in the basement of his house, which was on South Main Street across from Charlie Gail's general store. Not many houses had basements but his house set up high and apparently was above the water table. That house is still there. You went to his basement door where he had a voice tube that you blowed into which tooted a horn upstairs and pretty soon him or Miz LeKintes would speak into their end of the tube and say he would be right down, or he is on a house call, or whatever. When he did come and open the basement door, you had to talk real loud till he got out his earhorn and sometimes you might say one thing and he think you said something else, with dreadful results on your treatment. Everybody told the story that a mama brought her boy in and told Doc LeKintes her son had swallered a quarter. Doc LeKintes almost treated the boy for rabies when he thought she said the boy couldn't swaller water. As it was, he laughed and told her to watch the potty and the quarter would arrive in a couple of days. Speaking of rabies, there was occasions when I saw Turk, the policeman, shoot and kill dogs that was foaming at the mouth and otherwise acting funny due to rabies being right common in them days.

Doc LeKintes had a powerful Hudson Hornet car, two hundred horsepower, I expect, and was killed in an accident up to Delaware where he was attending a testimonial dinner. After he died, his widder forgived the debts of his poor patients, causing many a Chincoteaguer to wish he had put his doctoring on the cuff too. Later, another doctor came and set up a little hospital in that house, mostly for birthing. I am familiar here as I helped the new doc by, among other things, incinurating afterbirths in a fire.

My tongue healed and I did get up the nerve to catch again but I stood well back of the batter now, as did pretty well everybody else when assigned to be catcher. Besides no mask, we did not have no protection for our manly parts, neither. Also, some batters did what we called "slinging their bat". Whenever one of them come up to bat, somebody was sure to yell to the catcher, "Watch out, he slings his bat." After a bat slinger hit a ball, he slung the bat behind them, towards your feet if you was lucky. Now I think about it, we was quite lucky the only real damage that summer was to my tongue, and regarding that injury, some said that for a while, my injury was something of a blessing due to my reputation as a talker.

After a while we got tired of practicing and Pete Cantrell, who had took over both managing and coaching, had somehow, without access to a telephone, arranged a match with a team from Greenback on the mainland. That team was all big farm boys, mostly older than us, but we had excitement on our side. Nobody give a thought to how we would get over to Greenback, we just waited for the feed barge that brought chicken feed for all them hundreds of thousands of fryers I told you about earlier.

There was a rail-head at Greenback and most things, and especially chicken feed was barged to Chincoteague from there, that being the most equalnomical way to move things back then. We asked Haywood Watson, the barge man, if we could have a ride to Greenback and he said as long as we was careful not to fall overboard it was OK. Take note the lack of lawyers back then made it more fun to be a young'un. We also asked him what time we would have to be back at the Greenback dock to catch a ride back with him. I recall it took about four hours to load the barge, it being done by Haywood himself, so we limited our big game to seven innings to be sure to make our ride home. The ride over was right nice, took about an hour on that sunny Saturday morning, and we docked at Greenback about twelve noon. The field was about a half mile from the dock at a school, making us glad we did not have a lot of equipment to carry, and except for the grass in left field, which was about shin high, them farmer boys had that field in good shape, a nice fresh chicken wire backstop back of the plate and fresh lime on the foul lines, though the bases was old and rotten canvas bags, and home plate was sawed out of yellow pine. Them big farm boys was doing fungos and practicing whipping the ball from base to base, and looking somewhat superior to what we ever looked like, and I could see the spirits of everybody start to sag when we seen them big sluggers, but Pete stepped up to be our coach and he set us to work pitching and tossing balls about, while he walked all over the field looking around at everthing and checking the wind by throwing sprigs of grass in the air. When he come back we huddled and he said, "Blue Jays, these boys look good but we can beat them. See that grass in left field? We will hit to it, when we can. Balls can get lost in there it is so deep. And when they bat and they hit to that tall grass with a man on base, our left fielder must cause the runner to go for extra bases by pretending he has lost the ball at a time when he actually has it in his mitt. He must take one step back to make the runner think the ball has rolled past him in the deep grass, then he can throw out the runner if he tries to stretch it into an extra base. We gonna put Ben Boy at pitcher, cause it will piss these farmers off to have a colert serving up pitches they can't hit. Ben, I want you to act like Satchel Page." Satchel Page was a lanky old Negro League pitcher who was being moved up to the Cleveland team in the majors, and would be the oldest pitcher ever in the majors. "Sachel is forty-two years old and has no fast ball but he gets 'em with stuff on the ball, sliders, floaters, and roundhouse curves," continued Pete, "and I want you to keep them farmers off balance by throwing pitches just like Satchel with lots of stuff on 'em."

We lost the coin toss and the farmers took the bats and we went to the field. I was catching and them farmers took pity on me and lent me their mask, so even though I had no protection for my manly parts, I eased myself up close to the batters where catchers normally squat and did a right journeyman job at catching that day. And my manly parts managed to not get hit.

The umpiring was handled by Lottie, who, because she was a woman, was able to stifle the normal arguments over whether a pitch was a strike or a ball, even though she did her umpiring from behind the pitcher, where she could also clearly see the field activity, as she was the umpire for both pitches and field outs and safes. She was also honest in her calls and unshakable in her decisions, laying out her reasons with logic no hulk of a farmer could hope to understand, let alone argue with.

Now, something I have not touched on up to now is the superiority that Chincoteaguers felt over Mainlanders. Looking back at it, there weren't no logic to it, but we was mighty proud to be Chincoteaguers, and like a lot of things said often enough, it begun to be taken by us as true that we was just naturally superior to any mainlander. So our chatter when we were in the field was mostly a reflection of how superior we felt. Never, "Let's get this man out" or anything like that, but more like, "OK Pete, your turn to have some fun. You take this out," and a couple of us might just lay down right there on the field and pretend to pay no attention to the game. I know it sounds crazy but them farmer boys started acting like a bunch of nervous Nellies, striking out when they batted and fumbling grounders when we batted. We were beating them so bad that when we got to the fourth inning and they were batting, Pete waved our team to the sidelines except for the Ben, me, and Pete, which was the pitcher, catcher, and fielder, respectively, and one, two, three, down went the farmers. Pete said that was a trick he learned from watching the House of David baseball team, which toured around playing local teams and beating 'em all.

More details of the game would bore you but we made it back in plenty of time to catch the feed-barge and even though there was nobody there to cheer us, we disbarked at the Chincoteague docks like heroes, and that was the one and only game we ever played as Blue Jays."

# Session Six
## (Recorded August 10, 1999)
### Gangs, Bicycle Thieves, and Walking Home After Dark

"Ready, Sir? I wouldn't exactly call 'em gangs, but the various neighborhoods on Chincoteague had young'uns that hung out together and did not take to young'uns from outside their territory. Ben had heard that the boys who lived along Beebe Road had set up a real big swing and they was letting young'uns outside of their crowd have a swing on it. So one day me and Ben and Lottie walked down South Main Street till we come to the Beebe Road turn and we could hear young'uns laughing and making other good-timey noises in the woods back of Woodrow Bowden's bungalow. We went towards the noise and saw just about the most impressive swing I ever seen. There was a real tall pine tree that had blowed over and leaned at a forty-five degree angle so its top was right over a glade there, and them boys had built a flatform about twenty foot up a tree at the edge of that glade, had nailed boards to that tree like a ladder so they could climb up to the flatform, and they was using that flatform to launch themselves across that glade on the swing. The swing itself was just a one-inch hawser with a wood stob which you could sit on with the rope in your crotch and the stob under your legs like an upside-down "T". They also had a length of fishing twine tied to the swing so they could pull the swing up to the flatform so they could get on it and launch themselves for a ride over that glade. They saw us coming and started kindly showing off by swinging across the glade and landing in a big pile of shats they had raked up on the other side to cushion their fall. After a time, having done just about their all the showing off you can do with the equipment at hand, one of them offered me a ride. I started up the crosspiece ladder to the flatform and was about halfway up there when Lottie commences "Graciousing" very loud and jumped up and scrambled up that ladder behind me, me and her scrambling up on the flatform more or less simultanishly. One of them boys was offering me the swing but Lottie was "Graciousing" and tugging at my arm, pulling me back from it.

"Gracious, gracious, Thirsty, those boys have fixed the swing so the seat is lower and it looks to me like you will hit the water if you swing."

She had whispered all that to me, and them boys did not hear what she said, and they was still urging me to swing. I almost did go on the swing, due to pride, but Lottie was so insistent that I said, "No. Maybe some other time. It looks too scary to me." And, though them boys started taunting me, calling me a scardy-cat, Lottie and me climbed down off that flatform, and Ben, Lottie, and me left, but as we walked out of them woods, I spotted them boys moving the seat to a higher position on the hawser before they started using the swing again, so I understood what they had been up to. Later that day, we was discussing the swing trick them boys tried to pull on me, and I wondered out loud how we could teach them rascals a lesson. Lottie, in her logical way of explaining things said we might sneak over there one night when them boys was not there, and lower the board on the swing, which would cause one of them to experience what they wanted to happen to me.

And so, some nights later, me, Ben, and Lottie made our way to that swing, and after making sure the coast was clear, I was ready to climb up on the flatform to do the deed but Lottie stopped me and outlined a sneakier plan.

"Gracious, if we just move the seat down to a lower knot, they will be sure to notice. Perhaps we should lower it at the point where it is attached to the tree."

You had to admire how logical Lottie was, and me and Ben made our way up the fell-down pine that the swing was attached to and found them boys had wrapped several turns of rope around that pine tree and all we had to do to lower it was unwrap one turn of the rope. Then we snuck out of there and laughed all the way home as we imagined what happened to them Bowden boys the first time they tried that swing. Actually, we never did find out for sure what happened but sometime later we snuck a peek and the swing was gone, though the flatform was still there.

Speaking of gangs, one time Ben and Lottie and me was to the carnival grounds when carnival was not on, playing in the horse race judge's stand, which was on a tower at the starting and finishing line of the racetrack around the carnival grounds. That tower stood above and beside the gent's toilet, an eight-hole privy with a high wall around it as if anybody wanted to peek at that business. Us young'uns was pretending we was follering a race with pretend spyglasses.

"Gracious, here comes a truck."

And we three ducked down behind the wall of the tower, out of sight of anybody on the ground. The truck was a flatbed and it had a big canvas tarp covering something they was hauling. We young'uns peeked through the cracks in the floorboards of the tower, and we saw three young men pull several bicycles out from under that tarp and quick roll 'em behind the privy wall. After a while, they come out and bring the funniest looking collection of bicycles I ever saw. One had a red front fender and a blue back fender, and a blue frame bike had black fenders.

"Gracious, they have mixed up the colors of all those bikes."

And Ben whispers, "If one of them bikes was mine, I wouldn't know it for sure."

"Gracious, gracious! That's it! They are stealing those bicycles and disguising them so nobody can recognize one as their own."

Now I maybe did not mention that this being right after the war with Hitler and Tojo, bikes was in short supply and right apt to get stolen, if you was not real protective of yours. The truck left with the different looking bikes and Ben and me went down to behind the wall of that privy, where we smelt paint in the atmosphere, and noticed there was paint spray in a couple places on the wall. We all three went home and I checked my coal bin shed and was happy to see my black Victory Bike still there, and later, Ben told me he did the same thing.

The bicycle stealing business dropped off after a couple of years when bikes was no longer in short supply but two of the faces me and Ben and Lottie saw disguising bicycles I strong suspect they had stole later become right upstanding members of the town goverment of Chincoteague. Can't help wondering if that was a step up or a step down for a bicycle thief.

Now my ghost story: Ben and me had been to Pete's house practicing baseball. Pete's daddy had set up a pitcher's mound and sawed a board in the size and shape of a home plate so we could practice pitching right there in Pete's yard. Pete's daddy loved baseball and taught Pete lots of baseball things, making Pete a baseball expert compared to the rest of us boys. Pete had seen lots of major league games and he would look at one of us boys and say, You look like Enos Slaughter." Or, "You swing a bat like Mel Ott." In them days they had a special baseball train that started in Cape Charles and Cheriton at the south end of the Eastern Shore and stopped at ever town all the way up to Philadelphia where it let the fans out right close to A's stadium. Chincoteaguers caught the train at Parksley, right down the road from this old folk's home. For a very reasonable cost, you got transported to and fro and saw a double-header game. Pete's daddy had took Pete up there a couple times and Pete would tell us all about how he saw mister Connie Mack, the owner, manager, and coach of the Philadelphia Athletics, doing his work in his trademark flat-brim straw hat.

We was enjoying ourselfs at Pete's, and as often happens to young'uns having a good time, Ben and me kindly got a late start home from there. That would not have been a matter of concern except that Ben and me was walking that day, having started some mechanical work on our bikes which was in my coal shed, in pieces, and our way home from Pete's took us past the cemetery on Willow Street just past where you turn off of Bunting Road. I think it was the Beulah Baptist Church Cemetery. That piece of Willow Street had no streetlights, a scary prospect, but neither of us could admit being scart, due to pride. Actually, there was no streetlights along any part of our route but the two fearsome parts to me was going to be passing the cemetery and later, just past the back of the carnival grounds, passing an old crumble-down church that had its roof caved in, I think in a hurricane. Couple of partial walls on a little hill and couple of organ pipes sticking up through the tangle of vines and weeds was all that there was to see of it now, and I have to tell you it was a right eerie sight even in daylight, let alone a moonless night.

It was terrible dark as Ben and me walked down Bunting Road till we got to the Willow Street intersection. At this point we had the Greenwood Cemetery directly behind us, and about fifty yard ahead of us was that six-foot green wrought-iron fence, and behind that fence, the cemetery. For reasons I don't understand, the Greenwood Cemetery behind us wasn't near as fearful as the one ahead. That green iron fence just give it a spooky feeling. So we walking barefooted down the exact center of Willow Street in case something jump out of the woods and bushes on either side, and just as we got to the exact middle of the green iron fence, we heard a noise. Both us boys stopped still and listened harder. "Oh! What that?" Says Ben, louder than I wanted him to.

"Tweren't me." The noise clarified itself into a low mumble and we heard a bottle tinkle like it was dropped on stone but did not break, all of which noise was coming from behind that iron fence. I grab Ben's hand for company and that cause him to jump and scream, scaring me so I start to scream too, and I tried to get my feet moving but I couldn't do nothing but stand there, screaming, and Ben was like my echo, squeezing my hand and answering my screams with screams of his own. Then we both seen something shadowy rising from behind a tombstone. And it was cussing. And it staggered towards the iron gate directly front of us. I felt a warm trickle go down my leg, and for an instant the thought of having to explain to my mom why I peed in my pants overrode the present situation. Then, just as I was sure we was both about to be captured by the apparition, the gate swung open with a creak of rusty iron rubbing rusty iron and there stood the man folks called Tittlewee, drunk. We boys still stood where we was, still squeezing hands, as Tittlewee staggered across the road past us and fell down in the rushes on the opposite side of the road. We watched him for a moment and when he started snoring, we recognized the low sound we had heard coming from the cemetery before.

The scare was still afflicting us as we walked again at a pretty good pace and though we was somewhat relieved at having made it safely past the scary cemetery, we both knew the abandoned church was just ahead, and the thought passed through my head that we could avoid it by cutting through the carnival grounds over to South Main Street, where we could see the distant glow of streetlights. But that would be a long cut and we needed to get home quick, so we continued on and a breeze commenced to blow, and simultaneous we heard that old organ start playing. Not a real tune but an eerie note mixed with an occasional different note. My other leg got itself trckled down and I started to run. Ben quickly outrun me and we both runned to the oyster shell rutty road that led from Willow Street to the Dale bungalow. Ben runned straight to his back door and I did not even say good night, just runned on the tromped-down pine shat path to my back door and runned straight up to bed and tried to sleep.

Some years later, the Boy Scouts purposely camped in that old church and the scoutmaster figgered out that the organ playing was due to breezes blowing over the two remaining organ pipes, kindly like you gets a musical note when you blow across the mouth of a bottle."

# SESSION SEVEN
## (RECORDED AUGUST 17, 1999)
### Lizzy Bethy

"OK? We recording? Like most boys entering their manly age, I was struck with puppy love in ninteen and forty-eight. The object of my affliction was Elisabeth Tugwell, one of the high school teachers on the island. I never had her for a teacher because she taught the seniors and I never got to that grade, having quit school at age sixteen. In my dreams and in real life viewing from afar I saw her as the most beautiful woman, outside of my mom, on the island. She was straight-laced and almost Victorian in dress and manner, wore her blonde hair in a bun and her rimless glasses were always spotless. She was so straight-laced the state of Virginia made her the censor for movies that come to Chincoteague, meaning she got to see ever movie free and if she seen something looked unsuitable, the next town did not get that film until the nastiness was plucked out. Ever town had such a censor, and I expect the poor towns at the end of the line got some pretty snipped-up movies, what with all them censors.

Folks gossiped that Miz Tugwell had spent only one night with her husband, who went to Belgium in World War One and got killed fighting in the trenches. That fit well with my romantic notion that she was practically a virgin, pining for the company of a blossoming man such as me.

Looking back now, I know my adoring eyes missed a lot of the blemishes on her beauty. What I saw then was a pearl-skinned beauty, her golden hair primly up in a bun at the back of her head, and lips with the barest touch of lip rouge, always dressed conservative in gray, tan, or black skirts, with silky white blouses, some with frilly fronts, and black patent leather "sensible" heeled shoes. She often wore a hat, sometimes a pillbox hat with a black net veil that teased you, letting you see just a hint of her beautiful blue eyes, or sometimes she would wear a large floppy-brim Southern Belle hat, and in one hand almost always carried a pair of gloves, and in my mind just carrying them gloves made her a leg up on the run-a-the-mill Chincoteague women, none of which I ever saw carry kidskin gloves.

Looking at her with today's eyes, I realize she was not exactly ugly, but she was not exactly pretty, neither. Her golden hair was brightened with peroxide and ammonia.. She was just a plain but very neat woman.

About this time of my life I had started dropping by the pool hall across the street from the firehouse, mostly to watch, as I normally did not have the ten cent it cost to shoot a game. One particular day I was sitting on the porch rail in front of that establishment, kindly watching the occasional automobile roll by, when a particularly useless example of humanity name of Barry Gardner strolled out of the poolroom, stood by my side and asked if I was ready to play a little eight ball.

"Nope. Got no money," I says, figuring that would end the conversation. He was a low-down hustler, preying mainly on young unexperienced players. Even had his own two-piece screw-together cue stick he carried around in a snake skin covered velvet-lined case.

"Well, you let me know when you're ready for a game." He patted his Vitalis-coated slicked-back hair and wiped his hand on the porch rail, leaving an oily palm print next to where I was sitting. I did not reply as my attention fell on the beautiful Miz Tugwell, who I spied walking north towards town on the sidewalk across the street. I was kindly in a trance, watching her purposeful walk, her hip motions occupying the greater part of my attention, when Greaseball Barry says, "Bet you'd like some of that."

My jaw clenched a little, but right quick so's he would not suspect my secret adoration, I says, "Naw. I expect she's all dried up, not having had a man since her husband was killed."

"She was nice and juicy last time I fucked her," says Greaseball Barry, and I felt a rage inside me like never before, but I quickly recovered when I thought to myself that Greaseball was probably just talking to make hisself look good. I absolutely knowed there was no way my adored lady would be near, let alone let this animal even touch her. And I left the porch so as not to have to continue speaking with this liar.

I slow walked across the street and observed my secret love walking past the Russell Hotel and turning right, headed, I thought, towards the grocery store located in that direction, so I cut to the right on the street before the hotel and walked till I was out of Greaseball's sight, then I quick cut across a couple of lawns and follered Miz Tugwell into the store, where I hung about, looking at this and that as though I was considering buying, all the while observing her beauty and listening to an occasional snatch of conversation between her and others, when who walks up and pats me on the head but Ralph Wilson, an insurance salesman who was one of the G.I. Bill flying students at the flying school where my Uncle Walt taught flying. "Hello, Thirsty," says he, but without waiting for an answer, walks over to Miz Tugwell and engages her in almost unaudible conversation, so I edged a little closer and looked at the radishes while mentally blocking out every noise except what Ralph, who in my mind was only a short step up on the evulution chain from the pool hall greaseball, was saying to my beautiful Elisabeth, which was, "I have my slides back from my vacation in California. Would you like to see them?" To which my beautiful Elisabeth, closely observing a cucumber, without looking directly at Ralph, but flushing red from the heat, I thought, replied, "At your house?" And Ralph, out the side of his mouth, not looking at her, said, "Eight?" And Elisabeth turned and took her cucumber to the cashier, and as she passed Ralph, said, out of the side of her beautiful lightly rouged lips, "Yes." And she whooshed out of there and walked real fast to her house on Jester Street. I was about twenty-five yard back of her but when she turned onto Jester Street, I continued on to my house on South Main Street, and after supper, I asked my mom if I could play with Ben till his momma and Big Ben come home from church on the mainland, and she said she did not mind if I did. I knowed Ben's parents would not get back till after ten that night and I went to Ben's house across the pine shat path back of my house and knocked at Ben's back door. I asked Ben if he wanted to play till his parents come home and he said yes, but Lottie have to come along. That was OK with me, so we played in my front yard till near dark. Then I says, "Ralph Wilson gonna show Miz Tugwell slides of his vacation in California and I want to try to get a look at them. Let's go over there."

"Gracious, I would be interested in seeing them," said Lottie.

So we went to Wilson's bungalow and could see a flickering glow coming from the open living room window. The house set up kindly high on a cinder block foundation so we could not see in from the yard but I did hear the clinking of glass on glass and it took me a while to realize they was drinking something. Then I got a sniff of whiskey in the air. I thought about asking Ben to put me on his shoulders but I did not feel right about peeking right in the window, so I judged the tree in the side yard was climbable and I managed to get up on the first limb, which was seven or eight foot up in the air, but there was another branch, kindly leafy, between where I sat and the window of Ralph Wilson's living room. Through the leaves of that other branch I saw something I had never seen before: Miz Tugwell had let her hair down from the bun she normally sported. That was a shock to me but before my jaw could drop, my gaze was caught by the flickering images being projected onto a fold-up screen. They was pornographic! Not the cartoon booklet kind of pornography you could buy in the back room of the pool hall that I was familiar with, Popeye and Olive Oil doing things dirty, but what I saw was real pictures. Ever time the projector flashed a new one up on that screen, I got more interested, so interested I was not paying strict attention to Miz Tugwell, who I did not notice dropped below my line of sight below the windowsill.

"Gracious, what do you see, Thirsty?"

I could not immediately answer Lottie, I just hoped she would not climb up on the limb I was on. Then, just as I was framing a lie to tell her, I was distracted. I saw, through the window, feet waving in the air. Feet with toenails painted pink. The bottom of the windowsill blocked my view so I could not see much lower than them pretty ankles. Then I heard Miz Tugwell murmuring, "Oh, Oh," over and over, and what with them sounds and the mystery of the waving feet and the enchanting pornographic slides, it was hard to pry myself away, but I eased down from my perch.

"Gracious, what did you see?"

"Nothing," I lied, as I looked around to see if there was a way I could get right up to the window and see what was going on under them waving feet. My mind pulled up visions of my beloved being assaulted right there in Ralph's bungalow. I spotted a couple of cinder blocks and put 'em one on top of the other under the window and hiked myself up for a closer peek inside. I was shakily standing on the stacked blocks as my eyes took in the scene: Wilson was between my beautiful Elisabeth's legs and doing what I call practicing making babies, him dressed only in black socks with garters up over the calves of his legs, his pimply arse moving up and down while Elisabeth was writhing under him. Not the kind of writhing you might expect of a woman trying to rescue herself. I was paying great attention to this puzzling scene and at one time I was about to leap off of them cinder blocks and rush into that house and defend my adored Elisabeth from whatever evil was befalling her. Then I got more befuddled when I heard my beloved Elisabeth say, over and over, "That's good. Don't stop. That's good." Them words kindly confused me and then I heard Wilson saying, "Oh, Lizzie Bethy. Oh, Lizzie Bethy." over and over. I snuck a look around to see where my playmates was. Ben was laying on the grass in the front yard looking at the stars, not paying attention to the whole situation. Lottie was jumping up and hitting my leg, asking, "Gracious, what do you see?" over and over. What with all the assaults on my senses, I was hypnotized solid, unable to move a muscle. Then Lottie said, "Gracious, why don't I just go knock at the door and ask if we can watch?" And she stopped hitting my leg and bothering me. I did not answer her question as I was still trying to get an unobstructed picture of whatever was going on that living room floor, and I did not see Lottie go around to the back door. I heard the screen door slam and Lottie's voice through the living room doorway, speaking kindly loud, said, "Gracious, Mister Ralph! Miz Elisabeth! Can we young'uns come in and watch the show?"

What I seen next was Ralph Wilson slipping his trousers on to cover his boney ass and Miz Tugwell scrambling about, tits flopping all over the place as she was hopping on one foot to get her pink lacy trimmed panties on, and Ralph yelled, "Just a minute!" to Lottie, who appeared for a moment at the entrance to the living room. Her eyes got real big and her jaw dropped open as it sunk in what she was seeing, and I saw her turn and run out of that house straight to Ben, tug his hand and say, "Gracious, gracious, gracious, we got to go home!" And though Ben looked confused, he let Lottie pull him by the hand and they run down the street leaving me puzzling over what to make of the night's events. I saw Ralph run to the wall switch and cut off the room lights, but the slide show was still providing enough light for me, kindly fascinated, to watch the hurried dressing of my former beloved. Then I eased down from them cinder blocks and slunk out of the yard and I trotted home, too. I had some strange dreams that night. My momma said I talked in my sleep all night.

Some years later I found myself in front of Miz Tugwell in a line at the bank. We talked small talk until my turn at the window. I finished my business with the teller and turned to leave.

"Nice talking to you, Lizzy-Bethy," says I. She shot me an arched eyebrow look that told me she understood where I got that name from, but said nothing, only smiled. She died not too long after. Like I said, I never had her for a teacher, but I bet if I had, my calling her Lizzy-Bethy would have assured me some improvement in my school report cards."

# Session Eight
## (Recorded August 24, 1999)
### Everybody Does It

"Ben and Lottie come through the pine woods to the back of my house and in the quiet, polite voice colerts used when around white folks, Ben said through my kitchen screen door, "Miss Leona, can Thirsty play today?" I come out on the back porch. Ben and Lottie was sitting on our porch swing, which was the only thing out there besides our icebox.

"My mom's at the tomater factory and pop's out to sea fishing on the dragger," says I. A dragger was how you fished for flounder or fluke. The boat dragged a net along the bottom behind it. Scraped them flat fish off of the bottom. "What you got in mind?"

"Gracious, I don't know. What do you want to do?", said Lottie. I never heard that girl open her mouth but what she said "gracious."

"Firemen already gone to Assateague on their hosses for the round-up," said Ben, "I sure would like to watch it. Maybe we might get lucky and find a parachute or something washed up on the beach."

It being only a couple of years after the war, folks often found stuff like that washed up. Besides the silk gunnery target I already told you about, I once found three cases of lye soap with U.S. Army wrote on ever bar washed up on Assateague beach. We did not have to buy store soap for the rest of that year. Store bought soap was taking over from homemade lye soap in forty-eight, though many folks, mostly the old-timers, still made their own, using the lard and ashes from their hog slaughter. A lot of things that are right common in stores now had not been thought of then. Shampoo. I never understood why hair needs a different soap than the rest of you. Deodorant. Well, there was Mum deodorant but very few people used it then. It was a little jar the size of a silver dollar filled with salve that women dipped a finger into and dabbed it under their armpits. Never heard of a man using Mum, nor any other deodorant in forty-eight.

"Gracious, I have never seen the round-up and I would certainly like to. How will we get to Assateague?"

Lottie knowed we'd have to swim or find a boat to borrow because in them days they was no bridge over to Assateague.

"I know where there's a boat we can use, but now's not a good time," says me, "Tide's not right in Assateague Channel. Be easier to get out of the gut to Assateague Channel when the tide there is going out. Let the tide help us." I always knowed the tides due to my daddy's work as a waterman. Assateague Channel was between Chincoteague and Assateague. " Tide in Chincoteague Channel still rising. When it is high tide at the toll bridge, it'll be about forty five minutes later that the tide in Assateague Channel starts ebbing. Let's go down to the fishdock. I want to jump off the top of the toll bridge. I ain't never done it yet."

"Gracious, I have never done that before, either. Do you think I'm capable of that? Maybe I'll only watch you boys jump." You had to admire how Lottie talked. So proper. I hear she is a medical doctor in John Hopkin up to Baltimore now.

"I ain't never jumped off it neither," said Ben, "But we got to do it sometime. And it's a whole lots easier at high tide. Not so far to fall." Ben was right about having to do it sometime. Everybody I knew on that island jumped off of that bridge at least once. You just had to do it. It was a measure of your manhood.

So we got our bikes and rode to the fishdock just south of the toll bridge in the middle of town. My bike was what they called a "Victory Bike," first ones they built after the war. Had thin tires and them caliber brakes that squeezes your rims to stop you. Ben's bike was built before the war. Had them fat balloon tires and what they call a coaster brake. You moved your pedals backwards to stop. Lottie did not have a bike. She rode with Ben, sitting on the seat with her hands on his shoulders, her legs spread like an "A" to give Ben pedaling space while he stood up front of her behind the handlebars and pumped the pedals. We all was barefooted. Besides being equalnomical, you never got a galded heel from shoes. And us being barefooted was a reason Lottie sat on the seat. Summer of forty-six she cut her heel nearly off in the front wheel spokes riding as passenger sidesaddle on the bar between the seat and handlebars. Had a white scar line across her heel, right where her skin changed from the dark on top of her foot to the white of her sole. She lucky she did not slice her Achillies tandem.

We got to the fishdock and parked our bikes behind Brashear's Gas Station, which was the first thing you come to on your right as you come off of the toll bridge from the mainland. I believe it sold Sinclair gas, seems I remember a dinosaur, which was their trademark, but I can't be sure. Josh Brashear had his leg blowed off in the first world war and that leg was now wooden. Not a pointy pegleg like what pirates had but his had a sock and a shoe and a hinge at the ankle and little coil springs built into it to make it act natural. He limped some but you might not never know he hadn't a right leg from under the knee down. Once in a while when he had on old overhalls, he kidded around with young'uns by saying he could not feel no pain and proved it by sticking an icepick in that wood leg, right through his pantsleg. Right scary if you did not know the secret.

Icepicks reminds me to tell you that most everybody had iceboxes then. Iceman come around ever day in hot times, and less and less as the weather cooled off. You had a square yellow cardboard sign with prices printed on the four long sides of it and you put it in your window or screen door where the iceman could see it from the street. If you had the ten cent end up, he brung you a ten cent size piece. Same for twenty-five cent, fifty cent, one dollar, however you had set that yellow card so he could read it from the street. Ice was made at a ice plant at the fishdock, that being a handy location for icing down fish in boxes to be trucked to cities. Harvey Means run the iceplant. For a joke he always said he got paid forty dollar a week and all the ice he could eat. Don't think Harvey could have made a living telling jokes.

Ice plant made ice by using ammonia, which was a kindly fascinating thing to see, too, but I won't interump your train of thought to explain it, except to tell you that ammonia was yet another of them Chincoteague smells that told you where you was even with you eyes closed. When you smelt that ammonia, you knowed you was on the lee side of the ice plant. And it simultanishly cleared up your nosal passengers.

So we walked from Brashear's Filling Station down a path of crushed oyster shells to the wood of the dock. Though our feet was tough by this time of the summer, we still had to walk careful, laying our steps down easy so's not to get cut from some sharp oyster shell. We three sat with our feet hanging over the edge of the creosote-painted dock. Creosote was an oily tar paint put on wood to keep sea worms from eating it. Course it's harder to use it now that the enviromeddlers took over the US goverment.

There was not much going on. No boats in sight in the channel. Couple of men standing about two hundred foot away on the other end of the fishdock having a whispery but animated conversation. We could hear talk by some other men in a room back of the dock. Always a hi-lo-jack card game in there. Not much automobile traffic on the toll bridge, maybe one ever five, ten minute. Not many folks had automobiles then. Use to even be a bus to T's Corner on the mainland couple three times a day so's you could connect up with the Greyhound or Trailway bus to go somewheres important.

"Gracious, there's Ross the bridgetender man sitting in front of his shack. Can he see us?"

"No", says I, "And what if he does? We hain't done nothing."

The bridgetender was the man who when he heard boats whistle for the bridge to be open, run from his shack on the other side of the bridge, the mainland side, up to a little cab in the middle of the bridge where he pushed and pulled leavers and made fences come down across the road on both ends of the bridge to stop cars, while all the while a bell ringed like a loud telephone bell, over and over as the middle of the bridge turned so they was an opening on both sides of it where the tall boats went through, then he rotated her back t'other way closed, raised the fences, and automobile traffic moved again. Another fascinating thing to watch.

Ross the bridgetender sat on a bench in front of his shack on the mainland side of the bridge, whittling chips off a wood stob, which is what Chincoteaguers called any little stick of wood, not seeming to pay us young'uns any mind.

"Gracious, gracious, I can't do it, I know I can't."

I don't know why but my gaze passed by where the two men had been arguing. One of them two men on the dock was gone and Lottie's loud protests got the attention of the man still there. He was looking our way, and you know how when you in the bright sun it's hard to clearly see things that's in the shade? Well, him being in the shade of the roof, he was just a shadow there. Only thing I could make out was he had on a slouch hat and gumboots with the tops folded down.

"Let's go. It's flood tide and I'm ready", says I, and we three run to the oyster shell path, where our running become slower due to needing to lay down our footsoles gingerly.

"Gracious, gracious, slow down. How can I keep up?"

Ben and me stopped by the edge of the tar road to let Lottie catch up and then we run fast across about ten foot of that black tar road, which the sun made very hot cause it is black, to the white concrete of the toll bridge, where we stopped to let the concrete suck the hot outen our feet, and to let Lottie catch up.

"Gracious, gracious, gracious, I'm not sure I can do it."

Lottie started to fall behind and the graciouses started coming out of her pretty steady as us two boys run to the middle of the bridge to a rusty iron ladder painted silver that went up to the top of it.

"Careful on that third rung, it always been loose", says Ben, reminding us of something every young'un on Chincoteague knowed but that we could have forgot in the excitement.

Ben climbed up first, and I was close behind, with my hands grabbing rungs soon as his feet got off of them. I looked down to see Lottie walking backwards down the bridge, looking up at us. And I seen the slouch hat man in the shade was apparently still interested. He was still watching.

I can't tell you just how exciting the moment was we got off that ladder and sat straddle of the top girder. Seem like you could see everything from such a height. Also saw Ross the bridgetender took notice of us.

"You young'uns git down off of there right now," says he, moving towards the ladder. But he's not moving excited-like. He's moving more like he's on a Sunday stroll.

Meantimes Ben and me slid our sterns along the foot-wide girder till we was exactly over the water where the boats passed under. We stood up careful, there being no handrail or nothing to get aholt of. Ben and me held our arms out to help steady our balance on the silver-painted iron beam we was standing on, and looked all around, taking in the glory of it while making sure there was no boats coming, then we looked down at the water to see if they was any sharks or bullfish waiting down there to surprise us. It sure looked a lot futher down than it had looked up when we was down on the bridge. The bridgetender, making his way, seemed to me still kindly slow, up the bridge says, "You young'uns gonna get hurt, you fall from up there."

I grabs Ben's hand so we be sure not to land on top of one another and Ben nods at me and I nod back and together we stepped off of the top of that toll bridge.

Everybody I seen jump off of there their first time screamed all the way down, and Ben and me was no exception. It weren't a fear scream, it was more a "look at me" scream. Seemed like from when we stepped off of that toll bridge to when we hit the water the time was stretched out like I was dreaming. I watched seagulls gliding round looking for minnows and I saw little ripples where the breeze touched the water. Then we hit the water. It weren't at all soft when we hit, but stung right smart the soles of my feet, but I did not have time to say "ow" because an unexpected second pain hit me. That water had ballooned open the legs of them shorts I was wearing and hit me right smart hard in my manly parts.

This time I did say "Ow!" but nobody heared it, for I was going down, down in the water and all my "Ow!" was, was some bubbles. I was some relieved when I stopped going down and started up, and I swum upwards to speed it up, I being about to end my breath-holding abilities. Just when I thought it was going to be too late and I would have to learn to breathe water, my head broke into the air and I coughed and sucked in some breath. For a second, I thought Ben wasn't coming up when up he pops right next to me, gasping for a breath. We both started laughing to beat the band and paid little attention to the bridgetender, who when he saw us bobbing there in the water, turned and went strolling back towards his shack mumbling, "Damn young'uns."

He must have seen hundreds of young'uns do that jump, for just about everybody did it once as a matter of pride. Bridgetender prob'ly did it his self. Some older boys showed off to the girls by headfirst diving off of that bridge. I don't know what that water would hurt more, top of a diver's head or a jumper's manly parts.

We swum easy over to the fishdock to where Lottie waited, and after me straightening out my manly parts under water and checking for damage down there, Ben and me climbed up an automobile tire tied there as a boat bumper and laid back on them creosote-treated boards to let the sun dry us some. After I got over feeling like a brave hero, I looked around to see if there was anybody who had admired my jump. The slouch hat and gumboots man in the dark was gone. They was nobody on the dock but us children.

"That sure felt good to do, even though it sure stung my stern", said Ben.

"You lucky." says I."

# Session Nine
## (Recorded August 31, 1999)
### Assateague

"Sir, I'm ready. When I left off the last time we had jumped off of the toll bridge and was laying on the fishdock behind Josh Brashear's filling station. We laid there on the dock for a time and had reached the steaming stage of drying out when Ben says, "Les go. We can dry on our way to Assateague."

Tide in Assateague Channel would be favorable for us to cross shortly, so I agreed. We got our bikes from back of Brashear's filling station and pedaled through the main part of town north to Church Street, and east on Church Street towards Piney Island, which I think weren't an island at all, but a peninsular, but it was a real short way to get to Assateague, the channel being pinched at that place.

Around the bend in the road after we passed the Mechanics Cemetery, we turned off Church Street onto a crushed oyster shell rutty road and rode east till on Piney Island the road turned to sand, in which my skinny Victory Bike tires got mired immediately and I had to dismount and walk my bike. Ben's big fat balloon tires let him go a little futher but Lottie's extra weight soon bogged him down too, and then we all was walking. We walked on that sand road to a dock where I knowed there was a bateau we could use. It did have about six inch of rainwater in it, on top of which was floating an eight foot oar and a bailing scoop made out of wood. We left our bikes leaning on a dock piling and I jumped in the bateau and started bailing 'er out.

"Gracious, are you going to steal this boat? I can't be a part of that."

I kept on bailing. "We ain't stealing. This Corncob Mason's bateau. Game Warden Herb Brackalew throwed him in the lock-up 'cause he was trapping duck. I comes by and keeps 'er bailed out for him, and the deal is, he lets me use 'er," which was ninety-nine percent true. Only the "lets me use 'er" part was stretched some.

They called Corncob Mason Corncob on account of he always had one of them corncob pipes in his mouth. Them Masons was one of several Eastern Side families made their living out of trapping duck on Assateague, illegal. It was called poaching. Main outlet for their illegal ducks and geese was Chincoteague Island restaurants, though the occasional island family was also a customer.

"Gracious, you don't bail it out very often, do you?" That girl was always finding a hole in your story.

"You got to leave some water in 'er so the wood don't dry out, else the bottom gets leaky," says I. And there was some truth to that. I finished scooping the last inch of water, said "Hop in," and we shoved off for Assateague.

Judging by the sun, it was between eleven and twelve o'clock and I was easing Corncob's bateau out the gut to the deeper water of Assateague Channel. The tide was ebbing out of the gut and I poled us along easy, letting the receding tide flow work for us. Ben was laying on the bow on his chest drying his backside with his chin resting on the backs of his hands. He must have looked something like one of them bowsprit decorations on a pirate ship, if you could have seen him from the front, and Lottie sat on the stern deck, head swiveling side to side, looking at the scenery, ever once in a while saying, "Gracious", or just moving her lips like she was saying it.

Pretty soon we come out of that gut into Assateague Channel, the water getting deeper and I was about to run out of bottom, so I give one last shove with the oar to get a good start across the channel.

"You gonna have to move, Lottie. I got to scull now", said I. I guess you know what she said.

Sculling was how Chincoteague watermen propelled their boat before everybody started using stern-kickers, what you call outboard motors. To scull a boat, you only used one oar in a notch shaped like a "U" in the middle of the stern. Using only one oar made it equalnomical. This gonna take some imagination for me to tell so you can understand but I will try. To scull, you lay your oar in that stern-notch and move the oar's blade back and forth in the water back of the boat, making the boat move for'ds. But if that was all there was to it, anybody could do it. Problem is that oar is made out of wood and wants to float up out of that notch. The secret there is to turn the oar blade on each stroke, so the blade sets on an angle that makes it hold itself under the water, which makes it stay in the notch. It takes right good timing to do it right. I was real good at it. Not too much call for sculling these days. It must be thirty years since I saw a bateau with a sculling notch in its stern. There was a feller named Ganet who runned the mud digger, you call it a dredge, who invented putting a lead weight on the bottom of the oar's blade, which kept the oar from jumping out of the water, but he done it too late, sculling days was over. Outboard motors, we called 'em stern kickers, took over the small boat propulsion business. Ganet was quite an inventor. One day he surprise everybody by putting pontoons on his Indian motorcycle and making a paddle wheel out of the rear tire and cruising up and down the channel throwing up rooster tails with that rig. He was another right interesting Chincoteague character.

So shortly we was pulling Corncob's bateau up on the mud of the Assateague shore and I tied the bow line to a cinder block just to be sure the boat would not go nowheres. On some shores there was always cinder blocks scattered about, right handy for tying your bateau.

"Gracious, why are there so many mosquitoes."

"Sure is lots of em," says Ben, slapping and brushing his legs and arms.

"They won't be so bad when we get away from the marsh and into some breeze," says I, and we walked to the pine woods about twenty-five yard away, not saying much, just slapping skeeters and an occcasional green hossfly. Them pines covered a sand hill on the west side of Assateague. Once we got to the top, the onshore breeze from the ocean was blowing right smart, and we could hear the hiss of distant surf in the wind, and we wasn't bothered as much with skeeters. We could hear the engine of the Game Warden's bulldozer groaning in the distance. Herb Brackalew was the Warden. Them giant glades in the middle of Assateague back then used to come and go at the whim of nature, and Brackalew done of lot of the damming and scraping that made them glades permanent and made sure all them ducks and geese had a nice rest stop on their way north in spring and south in the fall.

When Brackalew come to Chincoteague to be Game Warden, it did not take him long to catch onto the poacher's tricks. They say the first time he caught some poachers in the act of trapping ducks on Assateague, he thought he had 'em with the goods but did not know they always backed up their bateaus in them guts that led to their duck traps. That way all they had to do was just slip their 40 horse Mercury sternkicker in forward gear and speed out of there. But Brackalew got his self one of them airboats with an airplane propeller on the back and he just cut right across the marsh and when the poachers rounded a bend on their escape, there was Brackalew blocking their way with a twelve gauge shotgun. I expect Corncob Mason was one of them he arrested. Shortly after, Brackalew was woke up by of couple loud bangs one night and when he looked out his screen door, saw somebody had tried to scare him out of town by unloading both barrels of double naught shot from a 12 gauge into his green game warden car. He did not give up, though, and between his presistance and something the sports from the city done, which I will get to next, they eventually pretty well stopped the illegal duck trapping industry, thereby making duck dishes at all the local restaurants considerable more expensive.

My uncle Walt also had a run-in with Herb Brackalew, which you will recall I told you about earlier.

Ever bad thing leads to a good one, though. Some of them families that was criminals then has done pretty good. They artists now. Famous for carving decoys, just like they used to carve to tempt ducks to their illegal traps. Only nowdays them city swells pays prices you would not believe to buy them decoys to put in museums for other city swells to admire or even to put around their house as nicknacks. Tell them city swells they buying from an ex-convict with a criminal history just adds to the price they willing to pay, so much so that carvers who are severe churchmen and never done anything against the law in their life has been known to make up, or at least hint at a criminal past just to tell the swells.

Back to Assateague. We walked southeast along that Assateague piney ridge till we come to a old falling-down two story house used to be the lighthouse keeper house. Cap'n Ben Scott lived there before the lighthouse was made to work by itself, not needing no keeper, and he moved to Jester Street on Chincoteague. Now what was left of that old house was grey from weather and while the uprights was still sturdy, there was not much left of the clapboards. All you saw was laths with no plaster. And there was billy goats there, maybe twenty, thirty. Their little round turds was everwhere. And being barefooted we picked our path through that area with care, avoiding nails, glass shards, and goat-turds.

Going easterly now, we left the house and the lighthouse behind us and follered a path that led about a quarter mile to another house, this one in pretty good shape. It was poured concrete with a corrugated tin roof. I peeked inside, though I knowed all it was in there was lots of glass lead-cell batteries that used to be charged on a diesel generator and put to work lighting the lighthouse beacon light. Another fascinating item.

"Gracious, will we be able to get back when the tide comes in?"

We had continued east from that house and was now walking through a kindly low wet muddy section of the path.

"We be outta this in a minute", says Ben.

"Gracious, when are we going to see the round-up?" Take notice most of Lottie's talk was always questions nobody can't answer.

The path here was through some reeds and bullrushes taller than we was, so it kindly surprised us when we heard hoofbeats off in the vegetation to starboard. And we also heard hoss snorts and the other noises hosses makes.

"Gracious gracious, Have we found the round-up?"

Just then we heard the noise of running hoofbeats and a man shout, "I'll get you, you sonofabitch." That could have been one of them firemen hossmen chasing a pony so we started through them bullrushes towards the sound. When we was just about to step out of them reeds we come nose to nose with some ponies that was fettered there. We was still in them reeds behind them ponies when our attention was drawn to a commotion. Maybe thirty yards away behind them hosses, on t'other side of a clearing was a man running back and forth across them tromped down reeds being chased by a man on a hoss. Through the legs of them fettered hosses we saw the man riding the hoss was wearing a slouch hat and gumboots and looked kindly familiar. We young'uns watched, fascinated and mouths open. The man on the ground was holding his own till the slouch hat hossman unmounts and grabs a big black braided whip off his pommel.

"Gracious gracious gracious gracious."

"Quiet!," I whispers, as Ben quickly put his hand over Lottie's mouth to stop her steady stream of loud graciouses. We eased down on our bellies, and laid there in quivering silence, not even wanting to blink, scart it might make noise.

Apparently not hearing Lottie, the man with the whip, after cracking it a couple times, loud like gunshots, snapped that whip around the other's shins and tumbled him down. Like a rodeo act, slouch hat man hand-over-handed his way down that whip, grabbed the other man's hands and looped that whip around them. When he was done, the man on the ground was hog-tied on his belly, ankles to wrists behind his back, with his ear in a fresh hoss turd.

Well, I needn't say how scairt I was, and it did not help to look at Ben for support. His eyes looked like Steppin Fetchit, bigger'n I ever seen eyes. And Lottie was trying her best to get a couple of graciouses out through Ben's palm clenched to her face. Next thing, slouch hat man threw a rope around where the other's wrists and ankles was tied up behind his back. Man on the ground was saying, "Lemme go, Frank. I swear I'll make it right, swear to God I will." I could not make out their faces, partly because they was some distance away, and partly cause I had my face as low to the ground as I could get it. There was only one man I knowed of had a bullwhip like that, other'n Lash LaRue in movies. I could not remember his name just then as I was expending all my energies trying to keep from doing my number two business right there in my shorts.

All of a sudden ever hair on my neck stood to attention when I heard a sound next to me.

"Gracious, gracious," says Lottie through Ben's fingers before, quickly, Ben renewed his palm clamp on her mouth. The man on the ground stopped whimpering. Slouch hat man stood up from his tying job and looked slow all around. We did not even breathe, we was so still. Then Slouch hat man kindly shrugged and went back to the tying, fastened the other end of the rope to his hoss saddle pommel, mounted his hoss, and rode slowly off through the tall reeds, easterly towards the ocean with that poor tied-up man sliding through mud and sand behind the hoss. Once in a while the man being drug said, "Oh Lord!" or "Please!" when he was flipped over by a hump or a rut as they faded out of eye and ear shot. We waited some and after motioning the be quiet sign to Lottie, we got back to that bateau in pretty short order. All the way running back, for every breath she sucked, Lottie exhaled a whispered "Gracious."

We got back to my house just about three-thirty, and we had a quick discuss about what to do.

"Slouch hat and gumboots man did not see us, but I expect he heard us" I says.

"We got to tell our daddys," Ben said.

And you know what Lottie said. She had not stopped saying it since Ben took his hand off her mouth.

My daddy come home about four and said for me to tell my momma he had a rough day on the water, and breezed right past me to bed. That weren't unusual as he got up around three in the morning when working on the dragger. So I did not have a chance to tell him what we children had saw. I fell asleep in my daddy's wing back easy chair beside the Philco radio. Mama woke me up at five-thirty, pointed me at a bowl of beans and pork on the kitchen table and said she was going to bed, too, and told me I could listen to the radio, not too loud, and to wash my feet, which I admit was covert with mud and probably goat-turds and hoss-turds as well, and to be in bed by nine. I did not tell her what we seen neither. Seemed like a thing I ought to tell my daddy. That's ok, I says to myself, Ben and Lottie gonna tell Big Ben.

So after I et, I went outside and washed off my feet at our outside spiket, come back in and sat in the easy chair next to our Philco Cathedral radio, which was tuned to a clear channel station. Clear channel stations was turned up to high power, fifty thousand watt, at night, so folks all over the U.S.A. could listen to 'em. I heared noises from my momma and daddy's bed indicating they was doing what I would call practicing making babies.

When our wall clock rung seven o'clock, I switched the radio on. The greenish-yellow light of the tuning dial was the only light in the room. After the radio tubes warmed up and stabulized, I turned up the volume loud enough for me to hear but not disturb nobody. I did not turn it on sooner cause Gabriel Heater had the news and then come the Great Gildersleeve Show, not a favorite of mine. I did like Fibber McGee and Molly, which come on at seven, but I couldn't pay no attention to it. I was glad it was not mystery night on the radio. I don't think I could have listened to The Whistler, or Inner Sanctum, the mood I was in. I kept remembering that poor hog-tied man being drug behind the hoss and the man in the slouch hat and gumboots. I went out to the privy and peed, a little jumpy at noises, real and imagined, then went to bed where I did not sleep so good for dreaming about the day's events."

# Session Ten
## (Recorded September 7, 1999)
### No More Gracious

"Are we recording, Sir? I was woke by Ben at my back door saying kindly loud, "Thirsty!, Thirsty! Come play."

So I slipped on my shorts and come down, stopping at the kitchen sink to splash the sleep out of my eyes and grab a sticky bun my momma left me on the table for breakfast.

"I'm coming. Want a bite of sticky bun? It got pecans on it."

"No, I ain't hungry" says Ben. He had his bike with him.

"Gracious, is it fresh?"

But she spoke too late, I had already et it and washed it down with water from the outside spiket.

"What your daddy said?" asked Ben.

"I did not have no chance to tell him. What Big Ben say?"

"Him and my momma was over to the Mainland to a church meeting, and Lottie and me was sleeping when they come home."

"So none of us told nobody and all our daddies and mommas working. What you think we ought to do?" I asks.

"Gracious, do we know if that poor man is living or dead?"

"Let's go look for Mr. Mitch or Mr. Turk," said Ben, "Police be the ones be interested."

That sounded good to me so we took off to town on our bikes. We got to the Municipal Office and leaned our bikes against the back of the WW II Memorial, which was in front of the Municipal Office and listed all the men from Chincoteague who was killed in the war. My Uncle George had his name on there. Drownded on a sunk Navy destroyer boat in the Pacific. Forty-eight was only two year after that war was ended and lots of people's windows still had gold stars in em, meaning that house had a boy killed in the war. Them gold stars gradual disappeared and, after a while, so did the memorial. I don't think folks was ungrateful, just lost interest in that war and worrying about their children getting called up in the next war, which would be Korea.

We went up to the door but there was only a hand-wrote note from Turk saying he was down to where the pony swim would happen on Wednesday, setting up for traffic.

"Gracious, what will we do now?"

"How bout Pop Ed?," says Ben.

Pop Ed was the jailkeeper and during carnival time, there was a good chance there was a customer or two in the little one-cell jail that was on the corner between the firehouse and the Russell Hotel. Or maybe one of the jail's steady customers, Tittlewee, might be in jail sleeping it off. He was called Tittlewee because when him and his brother was nursing their momma's breast, he always suckle the littlest tit. It was a very short way to the jailhouse, and we was there in no time. But no luck, nobody in jail, and no Pop Ed.

"Well, let's go see Turk where he is," says I, and we took bout twenty minute to pedal to Eastern Side, another of them names of neighborhoods on the island I told you about before. When we got there, there was a bunch of people kindly milling about near the shore and when we come riding up, a woman said, "You young'uns stay away from there. You don't, I'll sic Crackerdust on you. A feller found Pete Hancock dead over to Assateague and Digger is on the way to pick up the body"

The Crackerdust threat we knew was hollow, so we paid it no mind. Digger was what everybody called the undertaker, like Digger O'Dell the funny friendly undertaker on the Life of Riley radio show who always said the same joke on ever show: "I'll be the last person to let you down."

That woman telling us young'uns to stay back naturally had the exact opposite result. Us boys could not wait to see that corpse. Ben and me told Lottie to hold the bikes and we two worked our way through the crowd till we could see that dead man good. He look so scratch up and swelt up and muddy, I could not tell if it was the man we seen on Assateague and Ben shrugged to me that he weren't sure neither. I could hear Lottie starting in with low whispered graciouses. The policeman Turk was listening to something a man in gumboots was telling him. A man whose favor I did not know. Until he bring up his hand from his sides and puts on a slouch hat. That's when I realized he was the man we saw to Assateague who horsewhipped another man. It also come to me that he was the shadowy figure we saw when we jumped off of the toll bridge. I sucked in my breath but realized I was right safe, what with all them people there and even the law, so I edged close enough to Turk and the slouch hat man to hear what was being said.

"I ain't got the jurist diction on Assateague, Frank, so we'll all have to wait for the sheriff." says Turk, "But if you need to get back to the round-up, I'll tell the sheriff what you told me and if he needs to talk to you some more, we know where to find you."

The man called Frank nodded and turned and took a couple steps to leave when Lottie recognizes him, sucks in a loud breath, and lets out the loudest string of "Graciouses" I ever heard. Everybody look at her like she's ready for the crazyhouse to Williamsburg. Frank stopped his stride, looks hard at Lottie who is still gracious-ing, nonstop Then sweat pops up on his face, and suddenly Frank runs over to Lottie, picks her up by them hair braids with one hand, reaches in his gumboot with his other hand, and comes out with a chrome-plated snubnosed thirty-eight revolver, which he points at Lottie's head and, click, pulls the hammer back. First time I ever heard straight silence from Lottie at such an exciting moment, though her lips was still silently saying you know what word.

I looked at Ben, who got right tight-jawed and clenched his fists at his side and started towards Frank but Turk put a grip on Ben's shirt collar and brought him to a quick halt. "You stay put, boy. Your sister gonna be all right, I promise you." Then, still holding on to Ben by the collar Turk says in a strong voice that made him sound real in charge of the situation, "I guess you did not tell me everything, did you, Frank?"

"Don't nobody move or this young'un is dead," says Frank.

The crowd started receding like an ebb tide. I thought Ben was gonna explode. He was still clinching his jaws and his fists and I could see the hate and the fear in his eyes. Then Turk says, "Frank, that girl you got holt of there is this here colert boy's sister. Now you know how excitable some colerts get at times like this, so I am going to tell this boy to get outta here. I know that's all right with you, ain't it Frank?" and not waiting for a reply, Turk bends down and turns his back to Frank but keeping his hands showing so Frank knowed Turk wasn't going for his gun, and I heard Turk quick whisper to Ben, "Boy, you get to town quick as you can and tell Ross I said open that toll bridge and keep it open. That way old Frank there can't get off of this island without swimming. I promise you your sister will not be harmed." And kindly like a soldier, Ben turns about face and walks fast to his bike and pedals out of there real fast.

"Don't hurt the girl," says Turk, talking slower than before. I thought he was cleverly stretching out the time to give Ben a good head-start. "What you want to do next, Frank?"

"I need a car, Turk." It was hard to hear Frank due to the loud gracious noises coming out of Lottie.

"How about we wait for Digger to arrive and you can take his hearse."

"Shut up, girl!" shouted Frank. Lottie lowered her voice some but still did not stop gracious-ing. Frank turned back to Turk. "You stalling me! How about I take your cop car?"

"You know I can't do that. Chief Mitch would take a dim view of me allowing unauthorized use of that official vehicle, Frank."

Frank pursed his lips and let out a breath signifying disgust, put the gun hard against Lottie's head and held her so she was dancing like a marionette there on her tippytoes. "You want to explain to Mitch that you made me shoot this young'un cause you wouldn't give me that cops car?"

"O.K., O.K., Calm down. I don't want the girl hurt. Lemme get the keys." Real slow, Turk pulled a key ring off of his belt and threw it so it landed front of Frank at his feet. I thought Turk was trying to trick Frank into relapsing his holt on Lottie, who now had her eyes shut and her bottom lip was quivering what I bet was silent graciouses. But Frank did not fall for it and, keeping the gun to her head, lowers her some and growls to Lottie, "Pick up them keys."

She did, and Frank backs up to the police car and gets him and Lottie inside and after taking a moment to figure out which key of the several on the ring was the cop car key, starts 'er up.

Now I have been telling this part lots faster than it all happened, but the time that passed must have been ten minute or more. The way I figger, Ben must have been to Willow Street by now, maybe halfway to the toll bridge, maybe futher, but as the police car started to roll, I was fearful Frank might get to the toll bridge before Ben could get Ross to open it, so I used the only thing I had to slow down that police car, I thowed my Victory Bike across the road front of the car and for a second I felt only regret at doing that as Frank drove that police car right over it, kindly bending it all over, but it did get him stuck for a little bit when the car stalled but pretty quick he got 'er started again and he slow rolled the police car off of my bike and started moving again down that one-lane rutty oyster shell road. That road had real deep ruts and Frank was bouncing in them ruts and not making more than couple miles per hour, his driving complicated by shifting gears and steering with his left hand while holding Lottie by the collar with his right hand that also had the gun in it kindly pointed up the back of Lottie's head, when who come down the road straight at him but Digger in his long shiny black La Salle hearse with the Landau bars decorating the sides, chrome bumpers so shiny it hurt your eyes. It being only a one-lane road, I guess Frank thought Digger would get out of his way, but they both come to a standstill, bumper to bumper. Then Frank backs up a little and swerves the police car up out of the roadway onto the muddy dirt and went around Digger, spinning his wheels and throwing up a rooster tail of mud. He spun complete around a couple of times and I thought he might get stuck, but no such a thing happened. Then he got to the blacktop and went screeching easterly towards town, fishtailing the car all over the road, I expect due to the accumulation of mud on his tires.

Digger stopped the hearse next to Turk. "Where's the deceased?" he asked through the rolled down hearse window, but Turk did not answer, just open the door, pulled poor Digger out, saying, "Get out, I need your car," and Turk jumped in the hearse.

"Take it easy, Turk, this my bee-reevment suit." says Digger, smoothing the wrinkles, real and imagined, that Turk had caused in Digger's lapels. Turk did not pay no mind to Digger. He was turning that hearse around and in the process he backed 'er up right to where I was standing and I got one of them unresistable urges and opened that hearse back door and jumped right in. And we went slipping, sliding, and screeching towards town, too. Bouncing around there in corpse territory, I realized I found yet another smell that told you exactly where you was. Ain't nothing smells like the inside of a hearse, a sickening mixture of sweet flowers and formalderhide 'balming fluid.

I was straining to see out the windows if we passed Ben but corpse compartment hearse windows is made for looking decorative, not looking out of, having flowers and scrolls etched in the glass, so I could not be sure if Ben had made it to the bridge in time. Soon we made it to the toll bridge and I jumped out as soon as Turk screeched the LaSalle to a stop in front of Brashure's filling station. I felt good to see that Ben had made it in time to get Ross the bridgetender to open the bridge, and the town police car was sitting on the island side of the iron fence that comes down when the bridge opens. Eight or ten city swell's cars was stopped on the mainland side, and there was some cars stuck on the island side too. I did not see Lottie or Slouch Hat Man right away 'cause I was looking at the police car, but then I spotted 'em up on the toll bridge right up to the edge of the opening where the tall boats goes through. Slouch Hat Man was holding Lottie by the braids of her hair so she was up on tippy-toe, like a barefooted ballet dancer.

He shakes Lottie like a rag doll and hollers to Ross the bridgetender, "Close this bridge and let me across or she gets it."

Turk, standing all alone in front of the police car, turns to the people behind him and says, "You folks all stay well back. There may be some shooting." Then he turns to Slouch Hat Man, who is moving Lottie to keep her between Turk and hisself, and hollers, "Give it up, Frank, you just making it worser on yourself." Had to admire the way Turk's confident tone made it seem like him, not Slouch Hat Man was in charge.

And Slouch Hat Man hollers back over his shoulder at the bridge tender's control cab, "Ross, you close this bridge, now."

I don't think Ross the bridgetender heard him, as he did not answer and he was ducked down behind the iron door of the bridge control cab, just his eyes peeking above that protection.

Turk real slow takes his long barrel pistol out of the holster and holds it alongside his pantsleg, and hollers, "Lottie, you listen to me. I am an excellent shot. I am going to put a bullet into old Frank there, and when I do, he will relax his grip on you. When you feel his holt on you relax, you jump into the water, because I will be pumping lead into old Frank from down here and I don't want you in my line of fire."

Frank's mouth curled up in a knowing smile and he laughed, "Turk, I know something you don't. This young'un won't jump. She scairt to death of jumping in the water. I saw her try it the other day and she can't do it. Here, I'll show you."

Turk slow raised his long barrel pistol and pointed it at Frank, who backed up to behind a concrete bridge post which give him some, but not total protection from Turk's line of fire, and he held Lottie at arm's length, right at the edge of the bridge. Lottie was kindly fighting his pushing her, though with some diffuculty due to her being on her tippy-toes, and I heard her commence another unending string of "Graciouses," stopping occasionally to suck in a breath, and even getting in an extra "Gracious" or two on the intake. That seemed to embolden Frank, who grins an ugly smile and lets Lottie's feet get full down on the concrete. At that moment, a noise like thunder exploded right in my ear, and Frank's hand that was holding Lottie's braids opened and kindly jerked up in the air, dropping Lottie who landed in a squatting pose right at the edge of the bridge opening, waving her arms to keep from losing her balance and falling in the water.

Turk takes about three steps forwards, drops to one knee, and with his revolver steadied by his elbow on his knee, hollers, "Now, Lottie, jump right now."

Just like the slow motion I told you about when I soloed the Tee-Cart and when Ben and me jumped off of the top of that toll bridge, everthing slowed down from that point on. I could see a breeze rippling the water, seagulls in the distance gliding around, even a bullfish sunning hisself as he floated down the channel with the tide, and Turk's long barrel gun's hammer racheting back as his finger slow squeezed the trigger. Lottie had stood up and was standing with her toes at the edge of the opening, looking down at the water, mumbling "Gracious" to beat the band. Her shorts was pulled up in her crotch, probably from Frank's jerking her around and she looked like a deer caught in somebody's headlights, hypnotized. Though my right ear was still ringing from the noise of Turk's gunshot, out of my left ear I could hear Ben and Turk, and several of the crowd that by now had come up closer, all chanting, "Jump, jump, jump."

Frank's left arm he had been holding Lottie with was hanging limp and his light blue chambray shirt was turning red around his left shoulder. He turned his gun towards Lottie, whose eyes by now was open like a hoot owl's. Just as Frank's gun pointed at her, she hollered "Gracious" like a paratrooper might holler "Geronimo," and she *dives* off of that toll bridge!

Frank got off a wild shot in her direction and Turk empties his revolver, five fast shots, into Frank, who drops his snubnose pistol which clatters on the concrete. Frank staggers around for a couple of seconds and falls hard. A crowd of us rushed up there, led by Turk, who feels Frank's neck for a heartpulse, says, "Dead", and it comes to us all at once to check on Lottie, so we all run over to the place where Lottie dove from and Ross the bridgetender said, "There she is. She's OK" and pointed at where she was bobbing in the water.

"You OK?" hollered Turk at her.

"I am just fine," answers Lottie, as she swum to the fishdock like an Esther Williams movie, real precise strokes. And that was first time I ever heard her just come right out and say something without putting a "gracious" or two in front of it. And far as I recall, she never used the word "gracious" in that manner again.

Ben and me run over to the fishdock and worked our way through the crowd that was helping Lottie out of the water.

"You boys jumped but I *dived*. When you boys going to *dive*?" asked Lottie almost as soon as her feet hit the creosote on the dock.

"Maybe next year," says Ben.

"Gracious", I says."

## The End

# Epilogue

▼

That was the last of Thurston Watson's narrations. I regret greatly not recording him more frequently, for he surely had many more tales to weave. I miss my meetings with him; they were the high point of the oral history project.

Ed Waterhouse

0-595-29941-5

Made in the USA
Middletown, DE
02 January 2025